For all of those folks out there fighting their way through the off season any way that they can, everyone who taught me how to survive on the island, and Mister Milo Milosh

BETTER LIVING THROUGH BLOODSHED

ZACHARY VON HOUSER

OFF SOUTH PRESS

Also by Zachary Von Houser

Dreams of the Dead Night
The Long Shift/The Shuffling Night

BETTER

LIVING

THROUGH

BLOODSHED

BETTER LIVING THROUGH BLOODSHED

I was leaving town under the cover of dark, like so many shame-filled rubes before me— those sad, bleary-eyed bastards that had lost it all, just looking for some dank corner that would never feel the prying judgment of light—with a hole in my gut two inches wide. The lights of the Expressway rolled over my window as the city receded into the past; an island of nothing but hustlers and suckers, one always taking and one giving it away. I guess I now knew which side of the line I firmly stood on.

The end of the off-season, that point in the year when even the local money starts running dry,

and eyes start getting mean. The mop was heavy in arms exhausted from disuse, and my pocket was lighter than I ever liked; two-forty on the night side of the clock and I had made all of a hundred and twenty bucks. Sixteen hours of window-shoppers, over-talkers, and under-tippers.

I dropped the mop into its biohazard slop, pulled the little chains for the neons, drew the curtains, and popped the two deadbolts and the worthless piece of shit lock on the handle. With the music dead, a silence fell over the shop that, compared to the ignorable strum in the background for the rest of the day, always gave me a chill. There was something about the lower-than-room temperature and the smell of antiseptic that, without the festive beat of songs that you had heard a thousand times over, was always reminiscent of a morgue. The ten hours since I had last talked to a human being, or even uttered a sound for that matter, didn't help things any. I might as well have been a corpse myself.

I dumped the pathogen-ridden sludge from the mop bucket into the dirty sink, checked that the autoclave was off, and peeled the tight, nitrile

gloves from my hands. The dead streetlight bulb, as I wrote out my drop-slip for the day, gave the impression that when I eventually left, I would fall into the deepest space. Nothing was going on up-stairs, Angelo must be out for the night. God dam-nit, I should have left the music on. That place really creeped me the fuck out sometimes. A siren wailed somewhere in the distance, and I had trou-ble focusing on my math. A hundred and twenty. Half of that was sixty. What was three-twenty-six minus sixty? Fuck!

After a few minutes of frustrating mental in-ability, I pulled the phone out of my pocket and let the best minds of technology do the thinking for me. Shit, I was getting dumb. Was it the exhaus-tion of six sixteen-hour days a week, my age getting the best of me, or a diminishing capacity from too much endless scrolling joy on this very thing that was doing the math for me? It couldn't possibly be the sauce. I was German-Irish, booze was practical-ly milk to me through a thousand years of genetic alcohol dependency. The first O'Niell was proba-bly piss-house drunk when he decided a new name was the way to go. I killed the lights, and in the

brief moment of dark, I was nowhere. I was nothing but thoughts floating in the void.

Pacific Ave was its usual bank of dull-colored lights beaming pockets around the darkness-shrouded hustlers, pimps, and hookers. All of the shops—besides those equipped with bullet-proof glass or a sawed-off under the counter—were shuttered tight for the night; happy shop owners tucked away in all of the Dickensian garb dreaming of sugarplums, geese, and overpriced t-shirts. I didn't hear 'Hey baby, you lookin' for fun' anymore. The countless nights of walking the strip and careful rebukes had put an end to that. Even the low-level dealers and hookers were still eyes and ears. Be cordial, never shit on a free plate of food.

George was closed next door, with only a minimal amount of new graffiti on his shutters. It was all the same old shit, the names of gangs that didn't know better, a bunch of 'so-and-so-loves-so-and-so', with the occasional 'chink mother fucker'. The city really could be fucking cruel sometimes.

It was three o'clock when I hit Dead Heat. Its patronage was the usual collection of shit-heels

BETTER LIVING
THROUGH BLOODSHED

kicked out from next door. Bonnie Raitt was playing on the jukebox, and a bunch of downtrodden fucks were staring into their glasses, lamenting the pussy that they could never have had.

"Fuck off," Stimey said as he poured a watered-down vodka into a heavy-walled rocks glass.

"I'm glad you've learned your grown-up words, kiddo."

"Tom's gonna kill you next time he sees you."

"Well, he's seen me plenty, guess we should go in on glasses for him," I said. "Scotch rocks, please."

Bonnie died out to Garth, the faces lowered slightly with shame for whoever had played it. Stimey held back on the last pull of the tap, which I always thought was more grandstanding than anything, and I waited dry and tense for a taste of the drink. Christ, the busiest moment and the deadest were all the same, just unbearable tension just waiting to kill you. If I had just been some mother fucker bagging groceries. How good things could have been.

I got my drink and sat down, the horrors of pop country drowning out most of the pertinent

information that I could pull from these yammering idiots.

"Tom wants to talk to you," Stimey said as he polished glasses.

"That's an interesting hobby of his."

"He wants to know what you're doing here."

I pulled down the last of my drink and shook the rocks in my glass. "That's none of his fucking business, is it?" I slid the glass toward him, just before a pudgy frat boy with Jager splashed on his shirt could order. "How about another?"

That old killjoy Stimey gave me a three-fourths full drink and went over to catch the order from the date-rapey future-congressman, so I picked up my glass, slapped a twenty on the table, and went for the door in the back corner of the bar.

"Hey! You can't take that over!" Stimey yelled as my hand touched the handle.

"Tell Tom to go fuck himself, will ya?" I said as the chilled, salty draft hit my face.

I suppose it would have been considered a courtyard, by some scummy real estate agent hoping to get an extra five bucks on his commission,

but all I saw was a strip of piss-stained concrete alley with a couple of ratty old picnic tables that I would really prefer not to think of what bodily fluids varnished their wooden tops and benches. It did serve a fine purpose though.

In Atlantic City, if you sold anything harder than a soda in a strip club, it had to be a bikini bar. You serve a gin and tonic and a nip slips? Well, there's a big ass fine just waiting for you the next morning; or at least a sizable bribe to one of the fine representatives of the city, who were always diligently at work overseeing anyplace that could be considered even vaguely salacious. Don't get me wrong, you could in fact drink in any club in the glorious city, you just couldn't buy your drinks within the dim confines of their walls. So, what's the proprietor of a fine gentleman's club to do? Rely solely on the ones and fives that come fluttering down from the heavens, dripping palm sweat and all, to keep such a place afloat? All the while, watching the liquor store owner down the street get rich off of your work? Not if you have that certain mix of conniving ingenuity held by Lucky Tom, owner-if-you-know but manager of

Zachary Von Houser

The Ocean View to the public.

See, Tommy's a smart boy, a real innovator of legality. When he's not trying to find a new way to get the girls to simultaneously lift a wallet while giving a lap dance, he's figuring out how to do the forbidden in ways that skirt prosecution. So, can't sell booze in the club? Then just take a big loan from people you should never, ever take big loans from; buy the abandoned dump next door and turn it into a dump of a bar; throw up a big fence at the entrance to the alley between the two, with some Astroturf covering; and with the addition of a pair of doors on either side of the alley, the world's your oyster (old oysters in the sun being what the alley, or, I'm sorry, 'courtyard' usually smelled like). Still, he had a thing about beer being fine, but cocktails in the club were verboten.

I sat at a table toward the back, with a view of both doors and my back to the wall (a good practice for all of you up-an-coming hoodlums), and took a small sip of my drink. Stimey's second drink was always better than his first; I suppose it's just an old habit from being stiffed by too many "one and done" types on the tip front. Some

new-adjacent club hit was thumping through the speakers, but I had given up on club hits too long ago to tell you what it was, and this big girl named Janice was just finishing up her set on the pole. I think her stage name was Creamsicle or something else that was copyright infringement. Tom had thought that purple lights everywhere would make the place look classy—seriously, he actually thought that—but in reality, it just made everyone look a bit corpse-like.

"Coming up... she's hot... she's sweet... she's Candy! Everyone welcome Candy to the stage!" the emcee blared in that morning radio host voice that all strip club emcees have.

Short of the little cluster of kids on a bachelor party at a table in the front, tipping about a buck for the whole table with each song, the other old bastards scattered at their tables didn't seem to take much notice of the shift change. She swayed her hips as she ascended the stairs and made sure to face away from the crowd as she sat down her little bag at the back of the stage; a real pro.

I could smell him before I saw him. Tom had a tendency to do that, stink of cheap cologne and

slither up in a blind spot like a snake.

"You and me need to have a little talk," he said as he came into my periphery. I kept my head pointed at the stage.

"She's hot, she's sweet, she's Candy? What the hell does that mean, Tom? Is candy supposed to be hot?"

"How in the hell should I know? I'm not the emcee."

"Figured you were cheap enough to be, you do every other damned job here short of riding the pole."

"Yeah, that seems more like how you get your kicks." He slid into the chair across from me, the purple light catching the fake diamond stud in his ear and shining into my eye.

"Sorry Tommy, you're not my type."

"Alright, dickhead. You're not supposed to have mixed drinks in here, Phil. And you're definitely not supposed to be helping my dancers—"

"Jesus, Tom, you're not even the prettiest one at this table. You mind moving aside a little?" I gestured to the left with my hand, just close enough for him to know how easily I could slap him if he

got fresh.

She spun movie-slow with the back of her knee clamped up by the ceiling her hair dangling damned near to the floor. If you didn't know better, you couldn't see that little bit of dead-sad in her eyes, just the pure, money-pulling lust. Jen could really work the pole.

As for his hangup with my drink, well there was a vaguely good reason for that. Last summer some city council member's son (a different city with a different council) on vacation, got a little too drunk off of some sugared-up mix of rotgut and energy drink, and, when one of the dancers declined to take care of a rather pressing matter in the khakis, he smashed the glass on her face. Well, seems he accidentally banged his head on the door-frame a couple dozen times on his way out and suffered from a brain swell; the dancer couldn't work there anymore, because who wants to look at a dancer that looks like she got in a fight with a wood-chipper; and fuck-all happened to the dumb-dick security guards that weren't supposed to let the first event happen, or commit the second. Either way, Tom banned mixed drinks inside

as a sign of penance. He was still a prick though, so fuck him and his dumb rules.

"My girls are not to be working outside of these wa—"

"Thaaaaaat was Candy, gentlemen," the emcee stretched.

"What?" I asked Tom with mock confusion.

"I was saying, my gi—"

"Now, don't forget, fellas, Wednesday is ladies' night here at The Ocean View..."

Jen crossed the room with that blind confidence that you only get having walked a room a thousand times.

"If you bring your ladies, they get in for half price with free coat check!"

I finished my drink as she got to the table.

"See anything you like?" she asked.

"Me and every pair of working eyes in the place."

"Good, you're here too. Now I know what the two of you have been doin' and I can't have it," Tom cut in. "You read the rules when you signed your contract, Candy."

"The toilet by the V.I.P. room's overflowing,"

she said.

"What? God damnit!" He pushed off from the table and nearly sprinted to the corridor with the V.I.P. room, couch room, private rooms, champagne room, and every other dumb room designed to trick idiots out of even more money.

"Let me go get changed," she said and sauntered off with her little bag of too little money for how good she was.

Dancers get changed faster than any human on the planet, I swear. In the time that it took me to put on and straighten my jacket, and tip Galaxy, who was walking the floor, she was already back; street clothes on, her hair pulled back, and a slightly bigger bag. One of the dumb-dick bouncers—his name was probably Thad or Burg or something—was eyeballing us from his post at the front door as we approached.

"Hey, I wasn't done talking to you," Tom said as he stomped over, shirt sleeves rolled up.

"Take this for me, Tom," I said, handing him the empty glass, "hate for this gorilla to think my head would be good for hammering the door frame back into place."

And with that, we were out the door, Tom looking displeased and ol' Lurch not understanding half of the words I had said. We waited for a Jitney to pass, truly the most dangerous beast in Atlantic City, and crossed Pacific.

"Any work tonight?" I asked.

"All you think about is work, work, work," she said and gripped my bicep, hugging up against the cold.

"Money's honey, doll. Money's honey."

"There's just a quick run."

"Atta girl," I said. "Where to?"

"The shithole."

"They're all shitholes, darlin'. This is Atlantic City."

Now, I don't mean to disparage what is honestly and utterly my favorite piece of land in the whole, wide world, but God damnit the casinos are depressing. Sad shitholes one and all, with rivers of desperation running through their tar-stained, clown-blew-its-brains-out carpets. I have to give Jen that though, the setting of tonight's entertainment was particularly horrid.

I led the way. I had seen Jen handle herself

perfectly well in darkened alleys and smoky bars up and down the island, so there was little chance that she would have any trouble in such a hyper-secure, faux-seedy palace of indulgence, but I was getting paid after all so I would work every step of the way. On the ride up in the elevator, Jen applied a heavier coat of glitter and a long stream of some cotton candy body spray that damned near gave me diabetes. The creeps that would pay for a private party always had a penchant for that vaguely pedophilic shit. I just wondered how many times I would have to wash my clothes before either of them was gone good and proper.

She double-checked the number on a scrap of paper as we stood outside the door, her hand trembling slightly, so when her eyes came up to meet mine, I gave her a little smirk of confidence. This wasn't the first rodeo for either of us; this was just the ceremony now. Everything would go as smooth as can be, and on the off chance that it didn't, well, that's why I was there. A little spark of self-assurance lit in her eyes, and I stepped to the side as she slipped in the door.

There was no click as the door closed, because

that was part of our contingency plan. She told the client that he should leave the door open, for the sake of "privacy", and when she closed the door behind her, the cardboard back of a match pack would stop the latch from catching. Should there be any trouble, it wouldn't do to have me knock and wait. We were lucky that trouble was few and far between, but it wasn't unheard of.

Now, you might be asking yourself, what kind of sly maneuvers did we pull to get away with such flagrant disregard for rules or law? And the answer to that is, fuck all. We didn't have to do a God damned thing, because according to both us and the casino, it was a mutually beneficial relationship.

They didn't have to overtly advertise the company of ladies as a part of their service menu, and we had scores of rooms available, for a song at this time of year, and an endless sea of lonely, shoobie clientele day or night. If one of our clients got a little out of hand, well, they probably would have gotten out of hand on the casino floor anyway, and they had me to handle it instead of one of their own guards. No need to negotiate that type

of job description in the union contracts, no need to call Johnny Law after an altercation, as they would have had to during any other physical

incident. It's not like the client was going to call the cops afterward—there were too many unknown variables at play for a tourist, the local laws regarding such financial interactions, whether it would get back to their wives and kids, and there were always wives and kids. Letting me handle my business, so long as I kept it as brief and quiet as I always did, was nothing but a benefit to the casino. Plus, and the most important detail in the eyes of the casino, a happy, relaxed gambler is a stupid gambler. Well, more stupid than usual. They're going to play loose, they're going to play fast, and they're going to tip more generously, because they have the false sense that they are King Shit. They came down to this little seaside den of ill repute and were treated as the king they are. Wrong, wrong, wrong.

Our town always was, and always shall be, a steady flowing tide of the hustle. You're either hustling someone or being hustled. And to speak of the hustle, you do it with reverence, capital H

Hustle. At least it has shown us some results, unlike most of the capitol-lettered deities. Just being treated well didn't show that you were the hustler in the room, if anything it should give an ice-pick-in-the-eye warning that you were in fact on the conveyor line of being hustled, and it was probably already too late to change trajectory.

I rolled an unlit cigarette in my fingers and followed the bloated seam in the wallpaper from floor to ceiling, half to stave away boredom, half to kill the urge for a smoke; the guards would overlook most of our work, but there was under no circumstances smoking in the hall. One puff and I would be out on my ear into Pacific Avenue. Something in the hue of brown-red was smeared along the baseboard for a good three feet. Man, Jen was right, this place really was a shithole. Though she usually was right, so I wasn't too surprised.

A muffled shout from Jen, and then one of a deeper register, came from the room and pulled me away from my examination of smears and stains. I quietly entered the room; if you want to remain in control of a situation, calm and composed is the only way to do it. Rush in hot-headed,

without a full understanding of the circumstances or surroundings? Well, that's how you get yourself fucked up.

"Let's stay calm now, hun," Jen said.

He was about average height, a little extra weight around the waist putting his age past mid-life, a little bald spot beginning its conquest of the crown of his head shining in the overhead light. Jen had her back to the far wall, which kept his back to me, and I was about halfway across the room before he even knew I was there. The red fell from his face, to be replaced by the typical 'but I thought I was king' shocked betrayal of a rube.

"Okay, okay," I said, slowing my approach, but not stopping. "What's going on here?" Baldie started to speak, but I put my hand up. He'd be an easy one. "Her."

He turned his attention to Jen, and I continued my advance. "This cheapskate doesn't want to tip," she said.

"Tip?" he shouted, and I was two feet away. "This whore doesn't even put out, and I'm supposed to tip?"

My shin put out the backs of his knees before

he'd even finished the P sound, and he was down and flustered. I grabbed the collar of his cheap dress shirt and hoisted him nearly to standing, but still just off balance.

"The lady's a stripper, not a whore as you so eloquently put it," I said, twisting the collar a little to put the shock in. "She strips, you tip. You wanna keep those hands working to tip, I'd suggest doing so. Understood?"

He let out a rasping whisper.

"What was that? I can't understand ya."

I tightened the twist, his eyes went all red and watery, and his hands went up to my cuffs.

"Oh, my apologies," I said releasing my grasp, and he hit the floor in a way that made him wish he had splurged for a room with thicker carpet. "Tip the lady now, before I get upset."

He pulled his wallet from his back pocket; some cheap thing that almost made me feel bad for taking his cash. Almost. Five twenties came out crumpled in a shaking fist. When neither of us moved, he was smart enough to know to go back for more. The emergence of a pair of allusive hundreds got Jen's feet working and she plucked the

wad from his grasp with as much contempt as I've ever seen. She was out the door without a word, me watching her go as baldie panted at my knees.

"Pleasure," I said and turned slow on my heels.

"You know, you didn't have to be so hard on the little shit," Jen said as we walked down the boardwalk.

The boards were damp and quiet and the rumble of the surf sounded like a crowd of whispers in the dark. Before us was only the vacant gap of a thousand ghosts, doors lined with bulbs working the end of their shift, speakers telling only us the same advertisements that we had heard a hundred times over. A mist hung in the air and I couldn't tell if it was from the crash of waves or approaching dawn.

"What do you mean?" I asked, feeling her squeeze up on my arm a little harder.

"Why'd you rough him up so bad? You're never that hard on 'em."

"Of course I am."

"I thought his eyes were gonna pop," she said, with a twinge of something in her voice that

sounded like it could have been excitement, but not necessarily of the good kind.

"Figured the bulging eyes were just from what you'd shown him." I flicked the last of my cigarette onto the boards, where it quickly rolled into a gap, and lit another.

The last of a cloudy night had rolled into the distance while we were in the room, and the dead starless sky spoke of a void that had startled me with its utter significance of black my whole life. Perhaps, if I had been born somewhere without lights to blot out the stars, I would have thought differently about it; now, any time that I was somewhere away from the artifacts of man, the night sky looked like a lie. There was too much of a sense of life in those twinkling lights, too much of a chance for something more.

We cut off of the boards just past the old convention center, I know that it's Boardwalk Hall, but it will always be the convention center and the convention center will always be the train station. You just can't change some things on the island. The streets that lead from the boardwalk to Pacific are some of the loneliest places that you'll find

there. While there are some streets and whole neighborhoods that are rougher, worse, more intentionally neglected, you'll never find any on the island that are more forgotten. Plastic bags, old soda cups, and crack vials crunched under our feet as we left the ramp, the whole width of the city visible to us, the whole width of the world.

The city was in that strange quiet of the too-late night. The drunks were already sleeping it off, and the predators that would usually prey upon them were counting the change they'd scored; it was too cold and too quiet for the girls to work the corners and the cops were where the cops always were, somewhere besides where they could be useful. Jen had this dreamy look in her eye that I couldn't quite capture, but I tended to have that problem with ladies. Never knew what they were thinking until they said it. Had that problem with pretty much anyone, besides in a tight situation. There I could call a punch about to be thrown from a mile away.

I don't know why I'm yammering like this, but those moments of quiet in a sea of hustle, violence, and con have that effect on you. Only magic

could make that. A certain sadness hit me as we left Pacific in the past and the sounds of the ocean died away. No matter how many times you hear it, there's a timelessness to the sea that lets you know that there are only so many times you will hear it, and you'd better make 'em count.

Jen's street was quiet, as one of those rare blocks that are almost always quiet, as we walked down the little, gravel path between hers and the neighbor's house. Sea level being so near, a true basement in Atlantic City is a rare thing, but most of the duplexes go as low as they can for the bottom floor; falling feet outside of the windows being about chest high if you're tall and worse if you're not. We hit the top of her stairs, with a questionable deck over our heads, as was common for the upper floors; piles of tires, and a rotting swing set behind me in the weed-strewn yard.

"Why don't you come in?" she asked, the blue ambient light making her look cold.

"Never mix business and pleasure, darlin'."

The colors moved in like the tide, that slow-bleed leak of nether purple slick pouring up from

a barely visible horizon. I could feel the anonymity slipping away, that smooth blanket cover of sitting in the shadows on the sand, away from the lights and motion and action of a too-busy world, just me and the sound of those barely visible waves hitting the shore. Individuality crashing away into homogeneity, only to fight once more for freedom, maybe near, maybe far, far away. The first blues were hurt-your-eyes rich, warning shots of the day to come, and the ocean came to life. Color licked the crests pulling them an almost surreal distance from the shadow-soaked valleys of sea. Bobbing gulls shook the salt from their feathers and screamed to an egregious life. I tapped the tip of an unlit cigarette against my thumbnail, unwilling to miss the utter glory that my adjusted eyes would take in, if only I could hold out.

It happens so fast, that break of light working its way from Europe; everything goes grey for a bit there, like the day didn't want to bother, like it was too exhausted by what it had seen under its watchful gaze for so many centuries; then, just as you're about to give up, call the day a wash and pack it in, when the sadness really starts to needle

its way up, red hits like a bomb in your heart; the sky's all burning, the birds all sing, and that line of life slashing against the darkness breaks through.

Then nothing goes unseen. Every sin has a god to judge. But in that vulnerability, there's solace, because we're all out against the same judgment.

I lit my cigarette, setting the mood for the day, and a cool damp settled on my jacket. Still, the red in the sky hung as the sun rose higher. There's a superstition that that's a bad omen, and you can call that what you will, but for the working poor on a spit of land that's only purpose is to take the weather's abuse so that the mainland doesn't have to, superstition is the only thing you've got. Every day that the island isn't washed away into the depths is a blessing, and more times than not a curse.

The warm smell of coffee filtered through the cap as I crossed Atlantic, cutting the eye-ache stink of bus exhaust, mop water spills across the sidewalk, and last night's piss in the gutters. The corner boys weren't out yet, the casinos hadn't kicked the few patrons of last night to the curb, and a

calm peace was lounging on that busy street. Occasionally the worst is coming down the way, but it feels a bit less likely when nothing is coming down the way.

Her street was still in the hushed quiet, before the six kids under a roof started to scream, before the punishing barrage of a dozen houses trying to out-compete each other for the loudest music, before the brains kicked in and hangovers took over. This was Mary's time.

I took the steps in stride, dogleg brick without a spot of moss, and gave a light tap on the door. There was a sunroom, parlor, and living room between me and her spot in the kitchen but I knew the rule. A confident man never knocks harshly. The old nightmare across the street that had haunted me since childhood grabbed her paper, and a low murmur came from the dealer's house a few doors down—a twenty-four-hour city doesn't sleep in, even for drugs.

The door cracked with a soft, "We don't want any."

"Not even for your favorite nephew?"

"Especially not."

"Not even for a fresh cup of coffee?"

"From where?"

"Connie's."

"I'll begrudgingly allow it."

The enveloping hug and kiss on the cheek came before I had even closed the door.

"You need to shave."

"I've been out all night."

The 'tsk tsk, tsk,' was barely audible as we passed through the dim light into the kitchen.

"Cup of tea?" I asked as I handed her the cup.

"Oh, I suppose," she said, the kettle coming to a whistle as I sat down.

It had been a while since her girlfriend had passed, but the kitchen still held her hallmarks—a magnet here, an untouched coffee mug there. Outside, I'm sure a baby pool sat on its edge with generations of spiders making house in its innards. Change is a cruel one to let in.

"Sure you don't want a beer?" she asked as she sat the mug down.

"Maybe just one."

"That's my sweet boy."

A Guinness slid next to my tea as she sat down

and took her first sip of coffee. "Mmm," fell from her lips as though it had been a decade since her last cup of the stuff. Mary was always like that, not a sip for herself until guests were tended to. No matter how many years I tried, I could never get out of that 'guests' category. I don't think anyone ever could.

Your usual crew of watercolor houses, prints of tomatoes, and scratched off calendar hung on the wall, but the little details made her kitchen; an old edition of an illustrated Poe sat open with its binding up on the table, a beautiful martini set that I had mixed for her with since I was five sat on its rack, the plethora of magnets from casinos that family had worked at wallpapered the refrigerator.

It was good to have this routine with Mary, an anchor of simplicity in a world where that was in short supply. The odd thing was that I always seemed to fall into the childish routine of only sharing a rose-colored view of my life, take the good and hoist it forward, water down the bad until it's barely a blemish. This went on for about an hour, the sounds of the city now in full swing, Mary telling me things that she couldn't notice

how interesting they were, me just trying my best not to shock and appall her.

When she excused herself, as she did every time, I shouted that I had to get going, as I did every time. I took fifty from my cut with Jen, hid it in the drawer where Mary kept her cash, downed the last of my pint, and went out the back way. The back deck was looking a little worse for wear; paint peeled on the rail, and a few boards gave a sad sag as I trod over them. I would have to fix it up when I got a chance to breathe.

I started feeling the sleepless strain walking down Arctic, with its spattering of little shops, too far from tourism to be anything but utilitarian, and really started to drag after I passed the school and turned onto my street. In the apartment complex, I was either 'Blanco' or 'Flaco' or the elusive 'Blanco Flaco', never Phil, and I happily kept it that way. I understood that, even though I had been born and raised on the island, I was an outsider in a neighborhood that had been designed to be horrible by someone that probably looked like me. This isn't to say that I was in any imminent danger, or even treated poorly at any given time, I

was simply 'other'. Your run-of-the-mill case of, if I don't like it, I could get the hell out.

The little alcove by my door at the top of the stairs was the only spot in the complex with a buildup of sand and dust, just because I couldn't be bothered to give it a daily sweep like everyone else. I pulled down the note taped to my door on the way in and tossed it onto the little chipboard coffee table next to my chair. I opened the window to drive out some of the sad-old-lady smell that hadn't dissipated in the six months since I'd moved in. A sigh a little older than I would have liked escaped me as I dropped into the chair and picked up the note. 'FINAL WARNING' blah, blah, blah, '...negligent rent...' blah, blah, blah, '...thirty-six hours to pay in full...' A cool breeze drifted in the window and I fell asleep to the sound of too-loud televisions, an argument in the complex, and, somewhere, the sea.

Wakefulness came with a start like a needle driven into my chest. When and why this had started, I had no idea, but it was the norm anymore, these defibrillator mornings. I dug around for my

smokes, finding them wedged beneath me in the pocket of my crumpled jacket. Sifting through the field of snapped-off filters, I finally found one that had made it intact, straightening out the kink before I popped it into my mouth and lit a match from the table. My fingers felt like they had an extra quart of liquid forced into their casing and a phlegmy cough came up with the first drag.

I grabbed my phone to check the time and was surprised to find nary a message or email to be found, not even the normal junk that incessantly slides in throughout the day. Huh. I went to refresh my email and got an 'offline mode'. Weird. 'No internet' greeted me when I pulled up the browser. In the search bar, I typed in 'service outages' and was, for some reason, momentarily amazed that 'No internet' popped up once more. A flash of recognition managed to make its way through my groggy synapses, and I scrolled through older emails that were still available. Sure enough, a few days ago I had ignored one that informed me of an impending shutoff if I didn't pay for another month. One of the greater downfalls of a burner was the lack of automation.

BETTER LIVING
THROUGH BLOODSHED

The bedroom was more of a cramped storage unit than anything, with boxes towering on either side of the bed, like some old, lumpy, stained coffin. Even if I did feel the compulsion to sleep in there, a week in that claustrophobia would have turned me bat-shit weird. Fresh clothes obtained, after a quick shower, brush, and shave, I was ready for another day.

Mrs. Garcia was sweeping outside and an inquisitive displeasure was all that I received for a wave. "You're gonna miss me like a long-lost son one day," I said, which garnered a turn down at the corner of her mouth. I was really batting a thousand for the day already.

A group of guys were polishing a line of cars from the eighties in a grassy patch of sunlight and shot me ice when I glanced over for too long. 'Get your head straight, Phil.' Indifferent allowance wasn't the same as being welcomed with open arms, and even if that had been the case, there were hard men in every group. Especially a group that had been getting the shit end of life's stick for a touch too long.

A fresh pack of smokes in hand, I lit one as

41

Zachary Von Houser

I crossed the parking lot of the 7-Eleven and saw Tim coming up Atlantic. Tim wasn't a bad kid, or even one of the wannabe tough guys that tended to wander Atlantic by day, but he was a cheese-grater personality that, if I wasn't getting paid to work on him, I would never force myself to endure the punishment of. I cut the same direction as him, hoping he wouldn't be as likely to recognize my back, though you never knew with kids like that, and down the first alley taking me in the direction of the shop.

No matter how well you know a place, there's always going to be a little sliver that you don't know quite as well; don't quite have every broken brick, every piece of graffiti memorized, don't have the lay of the land quite within your comfort zone. This alley happened to be one of mine. I'm sure that I'd taken this alley before, as a kid or at least on some drunken stumble home, which had happened more times than I could comfortably consider, but not in any memorable way. It was a tight-squeeze alley, one of those ones that had been set before the first gas engine had hit the island, some shit-heel farmer's shortcut home from the sad, old

BETTER LIVING
THROUGH BLOODSHED

hoedown. The walls shot up on either side in that tall, featureless way that, when they were a bit too close, always seemed to be converging overhead. The one wall was a sheet of old-hay gold, with windows like pockmarks speckled along, the other was soot-smear brick that wouldn't be cleaned before the building was razed to the ground, the bricks distributed by the onlookers for the building of smokers, lawn edges, or to pass through the pane of a deserving shop window.

It was a pretty shitty place, even as far as back alleys go. Newspapers, dating as far back as the incoming of the casinos, had melted down to blobs of grey Papier-mâché that killed the corners and gave the feel that the walls were melting down around you. Vials and baggies sat half-buried in the green-brown sludge of old vegetable scraps. In such a small city, block by block it might as well be a different country. As I sidestepped some pile of indescribable, something that might have once been a rat or squirrel scurried across the asphalt. There are a few things in life that are unmistakable, and what I saw next just happened to be one of those things.

Zachary Von Houser

It wedged itself against an old dumpster, and I checked both ends of the alley for a trap before bending down. Sure enough, it was a genuine hundred there lost in the land of the worthless. A foot away was another, floating atop a sad brown puddle. At the edge of the dumpster, I turned and saw the benefactor of these riches. A pair of shining dress shoes emerged from behind the dumpster, bare ankles—a blue beyond life—showing between the shoes and the cuffs of expensive looking pants. Halfway between me and the shoes that would never see a scuff, a roll of bills were wrapped in a red rubber band.

I looked up at the wall of windows, the high sun painting them blinding white. Up and down the alley, not a soul could be seen. I bent quick and picked up the roll, pocketing it even quicker. Up went the collar of my jacket, down the brim of my cap, and down the alley I went. Calm but quick was the mantra.

This may seem a bit cruel, a bit calloused, but life on an isolationist island is built on mottoes, and one motto held court above all others. 'A rube's money is safer in your pocket than theirs', and

nothing makes you a bigger rube than being dead in an alley behind a rusted-out dumpster.

George had something from back home playing on the little television behind him when I came in. I couldn't tell if it was a soap opera, or a movie, or, hell, even the news. I'm not exactly worldly in those regards. I threw one of the plastic-sealed burgers in the microwave and made a cup of tea. I've always thought that green tea was awful, tasted like overcooked spinach to me, but that's all that he would carry, no matter how many times I asked, and it was the only place on my way that had tea at all. The microwave beeped its announcement of my upcoming disappointment, and I carried the steaming plastic bag by its corner to the register. The fumbling clatter in the back told me that Susie was doing inventory, no one could begrudge her clumsy attempts—I doubt that she was even of the legal working age—but it's not like I was going to rat them out.

"Hey George, how about you get some Earl Grey or English Breakfast or something?" I asked for the thousandth time.

"Hey Phil, how about you develop fucking palate?" I hated when he mimicked my speech pattern, but that was probably how he learned English, so I couldn't really give him any hell for it.

"Fair enough, but you just watch out when I open my own tea shop next door."

"Shit man, you take this place. Put all the shit white man tea you want in here."

"I couldn't do that to you, George. This place is why you wake up in the morning. So what's on the menu for this week?"

"Bird's nest. Very good. Makes you strong." Another thing that I hated was when he pulled this language breakdown act to make himself seem like he was full of some ancient wisdom. It probably worked on more than a few, though.

"Alright, alright. So what's in it?"

"It's good."

"But, what's in it?"

"You try it. You'll like."

"Alright, George.

He pointed me over to a thin gold and red can without a word written on it that I could understand. With that, my burger, and a big glass of

gross spinach-caffeine, I was ready to start the day. George handed me my change, which I threw into the pocket with the knot of bills; I never checked change from George because, although he could be a real prick, he was probably the only honest man on the strip when it came to money.

"I'll see ya later, George."

"'Ya?' Why don't you learn English? Country's going right to hell."

I pocketed the drink so that I could balance the burger and tea in one hand while I unlocked the shop. That smell-mix of A&D, green soap, and Madacide enveloped me like an old cardigan as soon as I stepped in. The door locked behind me, I tossed the burger onto the computer desk and sipped my tea as I checked the messages. Short of the telemarketers, and some tweaked-out crackhead that must have had the wrong number and didn't bother to listen to the recording, there wasn't a damned thing on the docket. My burger was a steamed mash of salt and chemical and something thick to taste a little like cheese. Sometimes terrible is exactly what you want, like you're some sort of future astronaut and it's been made just for

your particular deficiencies. Or maybe you're just feeling a little rough and sad, and the owners of these conglomerates know that the people buying them are a little rough and sad and got some scientists to tailor fit it to that.

With a little something in my stomach, I felt better about counting out my winnings for the day. One side of the knot of bills was damp from whatever it had rolled into, and the rubber band snapped with an unusual ease as I slid it off. I expected some show-off roll with a hundred or two on the outside and a bunch of ones to the center, but as I peeled the bills away and spread them out to dry, the hundreds just kept coming. About halfway in the fifties started coming, and the center was a short stack of twenties. A little quick math and I was more than five grand ahead already. After paying off the damned landlord and getting my phone turned back on, I'd still have a nice nest egg sitting around for a rainy day, and the island seemed to be pissing rain anymore. I guess I owed Tim a few drinks soon. Well, maybe not that far. I'd let him chat his fool head off for about a half hour though, with minimal grumbling.

BETTER LIVING
THROUGH BLOODSHED

I clicked on the neons, one of them part dead so that it said IATTOOS in half of a heart, unlocked the door, and turned on the overhead fluorescents. One of the flash racks fell back open when I pushed it closed because some dumb-dick hadn't used a level when it was hung on the wall, but I still tried pushing it closed at the beginning of the day every day with the rest of them. The ultra-sonic at my station hummed once I hit the switch, hoping my daily hope that I wouldn't get hit with any amps like I had that one time. I couldn't think of what I wanted to listen to that day, so I just hit play on the same mix that had been in the CD player on repeat for a week.

A couple of hours into my shift, my head getting a little fuzzy from the fishbowl life of seeing person after person pass without a chance to talk to a soul, someone finally darkened our door. She came in with an air that just shouted trouble; this unbearable mix of unbending confidence and an idea that, if she kept apologizing, she could run you around in circles all damned day. You tell any tattooer that that's coming in the shop and the door'll be locked in the flap of a hummingbird

wing.

"So, how can I help ya?" I asked.

"Oh, I don't know."

"Is there anything in particular that you were thinking?" I asked in a specific and general sense.

"Do you have flashes?" she asked and a razor ran down my spine at the pluralization. Seriously, and I say this with all love and respect, for the love of fuck people, if you don't want a dick hidden in your tattoo, or want a requested dick to look good, flash is just premade designs. Open your eyes and look at the walls of the shop.

"Yeah..." I said, unable to stop my eyebrow from rising. "All of that's flash." I extended a finger to the wall of flash racks that stood no more than a foot from her shoulder.

"No, not like that. I want to get an original flash."

"So, you want a custom piece."

"No. That competition show said that flashes are what people get. Haven't you seen it?"

"No, I haven't checked it out..."

"Oh, I'm kind of really into tattoos."

"Okay, then. So, what kind of custom... or

original flash... did you want to get?"

"I don't know, sorry." She gave me this painted-on smile that proved there was no god. "Why don't you just draw something up? You're the professional."

"So, like a skull?"

"Oh, god no!"

"Panther?"

"What?"

"Did you want to get a feather or a flower?"

"Oh, that sounds good!"

"Which one did you want to get?"

"Just combine them."

A little hammer thudded at the base of my skull. "Where were you thinking of getting it?"

"How am I supposed to know until I see it?"

For a tattooer that wants to be financially viable, the mask is the most important tool in your toolbox. You put on that not-too-big smile, dial in on a calm and positive voice, and retreat somewhere deep inside. That you that's talking to someone like her? That's not you. You're the little pool of molten lead eating a hole in your stomach. The you that's talking to her just happens to

be the world's smartest robot running through a choose-your-own-adventure script of 'good, caring salesman'. The stronger you make the mask, the more money you make and maybe, just maybe, they won't be a cheap fuck and might tip enough to make it all worth it.

"Alright. Just grab a seat in the waiting room and I'll draw something up."

"You know, on that show the customer sits with the artist while they're drawing."

"I'm sure they do. We don't... you know have much room back here. I'll draw it up and you let me know if you want anything tweaked."

Man, I hate television.

I spent the next twenty minutes sketching up a few different combinations of flowers and feathers that could work on an ankle or wrist. Call me a regular soothsayer, but I couldn't see her getting a half-sleeve.

"I'm sorry," I heard from over my shoulder, "but can you add the moon phases and get rid of the feather?"

I took a deep breath, and put the mask back on before I forced a positive, "No problem!"

BETTER LIVING
THROUGH BLOODSHED

The feather went to the farthest pit of hell, where it belonged, and out came the circle template to guide the way. Little daisies circled varying amounts of a circle in a way that didn't matter at all; then lilies intertwined a series of slivers of circles in a circle. I could hear my red pencil creak from the pressure. Another twenty minutes or so connecting two things that had absolutely zero percent to do with each other.

"I'm sorry, I know I'm difficult," she said with a little smirk like that would help fuck all.

Game time, boy. Come on little mask, I have faith in you. "What's up?"

"So can I get a heart with a heart-line next to it?"

"A what next to it?"

"A heart-line. You know, the line on a heartbeat machine."

"Ohhh. Okay."

Hold your tongue, kid. Hold your tongue. I drew it up leaning on the counter in front of her, the stupidest, simplest thing that man has ever drawn.

"Was that so hard to draw it with me?"

I nearly snapped, but that little puddle of molten lead just got bigger and the mask got stronger. "Not at all."

"You should really watch that show. It'll teach you a lot."

Setting up your station is a reverent act. Every action in a specific order, everything in a very specific place. Place things in the wrong order and it'll throw off your whole flow; anything in the wrong place and you're just asking for a river of ink running across your station the second you're not paying attention. Either that or a needle prick, then the next three-months-to-life are fucked.

I rolled plastic wrap over the shitty acrylic countertop of my station, taping the four corners down because I never did like the soap under plastic trick, and spun it around my soap bottle. The razor blade sat in the top left corner of the wrap, my machine in the lower left. I tore enough paper towels to do the job and not one more. A big gob of A&D squeezed from the tube at bottom center (coming from a tube instead of a tub because a case of tubes had happened to have fallen from the back of a truck and cost about one-tenth the

price). I shook an ink cap from their box onto the wrap and gloved up. A dab of the cap into the A&D and a hard press to keep it tight in place, a shake of the black ink to get it all mixed, and fill up the cap. The needle and tube, in their little sterile blister packs, went top center and, after I slipped a sandwich bag over my power supply, we were ready to go.

After cajoling her into a position that actually worked, no easy feat, I prepped the area and put the stencil on her wrist. She stared at it for that 'you're fucked' duration, and looked up at me with this look like I was some poor, poor invalid.

"Um, I don't want it to be purple."

"It's not going to be purple, that's just the stencil."

"Um, I know, but I don't want the heart to be purple."

"The heart isn't going to be purple," I said and pointed at the cap of ink. "It's gonna be black."

"I don't want it to be black either! I want it all to be white!"

"Okay. We can do it in white, but I gotta tell you, it's not gonna last."

55

"Um, my friend has had hers for three years and you can still see it. Anyway, the whole last episode of that show was a white-ink challenge. You really should watch that show, so I don't have to keep telling you about stuff."

Man, I really, really fucking hate television.

After switching out for white, I receded into the place where the molten lead hung out for the duration of the piece. A chimp in the first year of its apprenticeship could do that tattoo, so I wasn't too concerned. Five minutes later, we were done, and I started the aftercare with her.

"Um, I saw—"

"Yeah, if the show said to do something different, just go with that. Now I just have to collect from you."

It wasn't procedure to collect at the end, far fucking from it, but she had me so far into my head that I didn't know what day it was, so fuck it. Out came the wallet and she counted out exactly how much it cost into my hand, not a penny more, and was out of the chair.

"Thanks," trailed back to me as I sat with shoulders slumped in her wake, and she was out

the door.

Money's money, and that's the name of the game. All you could do was chip away a little bit from those who had too much, whenever you could, and hope that that would be enough to make it. Did I have a comfortable amount at the moment? Sure. But comfortable amounts never stayed comfortable, and the world was always pulling your cash away as fast as you made it. That's if you were lucky.

Halfway through my smoke, the door to the shop against my back to stop any sneaky devils from sliding in and robbing me blind—I had heard of sillier thefts that left people dead broke in the city—and my faith in humanity slow to try and rebuild, I saw Q coming up the block. I only knew him as Q and his handwriting was shitty enough that a release form garnered no new information. The kids playing hard would have had some knockoff, velour tracksuit, their asses half hanging out, and garish sneakers a size or two too big, but Q was the real deal; a nice Dickie's shirt, a bit big, but not 'dad's shirt' big, and pants high enough to hide the piece beneath his shirt in the back; a pair

of Tims on his feet in case someone got smart and needed a reminder to their teeth, and the regularity of their being new spoke to a need to dispose of evidence rather than some vain desire to waste money.

"What's goin' on, kid?" I asked as he stopped next to me and took out my pack of smokes.

"What's good?" He pulled one of my cigarettes from the pack and lit it with a butane torch.

A casino shift change must have happened, because the slow, rolling river of traffic was nothing but travelers in vests and ugly, little coats of gold, or burgundy, or orange, or the cheapest-looking green-brand-green that you've ever seen. Not a smile could be seen behind the wheel, so I guess they were feeling the same as everyone else at the end of what seemed like a particularly slow slow-season.

"Haven't seen you around in a while," I said.

"Money's tight," he said, rolling the cigarette between his fingers.

"I feel ya."

"Ain't no shoobies to roll or sell to. Crackheads don't got no one to rob, so I gotta deal with

them beggin' me for a handout, like I'm the fucking crack food bank."

"Got anyone joining up soon?"

"Nah, man."

"Well, when you do..."

"You know I'll bring 'em to you, tattoo man." He ground the end of his cigarette under his sole. "Alright, then."

A quick fist-bump and our routine was concluded.

With the knot split into two rolls, pushed down into my socks, and a nice little wad of it in my wallet, I closed up the shop with a glob of spit on the kick-plate. From somewhere above, Susie was throwing a litany of something that didn't sound all too nice at George, but I couldn't tell you a bit of what it meant. Kids these days sure were shitty. I know it sucks to have to bust your ass on the clock before you're even old enough to want to start rebelling, but you work with the hand you're dealt, giving shit to the people that love you won't help a God damned thing but to make you that much lonelier sooner. One of their lights above the store went out and things quieted down a bit. I'm guessing one or the other must have finally given in.

Q wasn't kidding about his game, though. The only corner boys that were out were the ones too dumb to realize that they were wasting their time, and not ambitious enough to go looking for a score the hard way. So long as they didn't start mistaking me for a mark, we were alright.

I'd closed up a bit earlier than usual and had an hour or so before I was expected anywhere in the world, so I cut the other way down Pacific. That's an easy way to get into trouble and a tough way to get out of it, if you don't know your way around enough to be able to spot the signs. Something bad was going down in a car just before California, a guy leaning against the frame of the passenger window, positioned to handle business, and the sucker inside all defense and shivers with his back to the rolled up driver's window. You never get out of a situation like that letting fear drive, it's always aiming for the cliff. I crossed over to avoid any of that nonsense, keeping fingers half-crossed that I wasn't in a ricochet path—but that's the sort of shit

you can never totally count out and can't control at all, so you have to make it the baseline.

Tony's was all cool and dim like a midnight church, or at least the type of church that I'd like to go to. The dinner rush was long since put to bed, and it was a bit too early for the out-too-late party types, but there was still a strong showing of the city's spread. The sad, old bastards sat on the sad, old bastard side of the bar; some young surfers clustered by the pisser in their surf-apparel best, even though there hadn't been shit for waves in at least a month; some tubby ball of Gen X was by the taps scrolling through his phone with a pout and the corpse-eyes of promised, but unfulfilled, possibility; none of the table-side jukeboxes were playing, and a group of drunken firefighters were fumbling their way through a pizza.

I ordered a Dewer's rocks, because even with an alright bankroll I preferred the cheap shit most days, and settled in mid-bar, enough distance to keep an eye on the door and far enough away from the rowdy clump to keep from provoking them into making a mistake. Without the time to put any money on my phone, I had fuck all to do besides

look at my drink and do some thinking, which was fine by me. Sure, that time on the screen helps you know what's going on in the whole wide world, but the more you distance yourself from your surroundings, the less you understand about the world that's directly in front of you.

A glass shattered at the firefighter table, and I wondered what they were doing away from Ducktown, where those types of shenanigans were acceptable. If you want to do shit that could possibly get you arrested, and are at least peripherally part of their club, go to a cop bar. The waitress came over to clean up the mess and gave a look to tell them what would happen if they tried to get handsy, and no brotherhood in the world would save them then. I'm guessing they'd been tipping as they went, and pretty well, or they would have been gone before the glass hit the red and black checkerboard.

A rerun of the news was playing on the little television in the corner, its volume too quiet to hear in competition with the main jukebox. There was a show that night, but I couldn't remember where and didn't give enough of a shit to think

BETTER LIVING
THROUGH BLOODSHED

about who might have been playing. A grinding screech came at my left as Gen X got back from the bathroom.

"So, where's Phish playing tonight, bro?" one of the surfers joked.

Gen X's tie-dye t-shirt practically brightened a shade over the headache it already was, until he he heard the laughter.

"No starving children to save tonight?" another cut in.

Those dead eyes twinkled at the prospect of a battle of intellect, and he turned toward me with a smirk, that sort of smirk that's so pompous it fills your stomach with rusty nails. "Neanderthals," he said, before exaggerating the sweep of his wrath toward them. "Oh, you're so smart in the safety of this... country." The word practically crawled from his mouth. "The plight of third-world peoples is something that you would know—"

"What are you doin' here if you care so damned much?"

I felt a slight change in the air, but the neo-hippie was oblivious, as they often are.

Gen-X Went on as if nothing had been said.

"It's something that you would know if you—"

"Something that you would know if you went to Lilith Fair. Why don't you sell your house and give 'em the money, you care so much?"

"If you knew the impact that... Never mind," he said. "Fucking meatheads."

The chair screeched, and things were getting rough.

"What was that?" The most average of the surfers, as they are wont to do, spat into his face.

The king of Greenpeace kept his face in his drink, the tremor in his finger SOSing.

"I said, 'What was that', bro?" The surfer was all veins in the neck and face begging for a tan.

Gen X cowered in his corduroys and turned toward me with a shimmer growing on his eyeballs.

"You asked for this, sweetheart," I said, watching the last bit of hope sink with the color from his face.

"Pussy," generic surfer said, tipping the scared little bastard's drink. "Sorry John, let me get him a beer. Seems he's had an accident."

You can always hope for the world to get soft for you, but there's always gonna be a generation

that realizes that it's a lot easier to make it if you get hard instead. Cry into your sleeve all you want, once the new tribe comes through, the only attention you'll be getting is the bad kind. When you've made a life of grandstanding for big ideas while doing nothing about it, it's hard to eat the truth when you're no longer in vogue and life is a never-ending cycle of harbingers of peace and violence. Something that fucks the fairness of the cycle, the hard are fine with times getting tough for them. The soft? Not so much.

One problem is, no matter how much these soft-as-pudding, old tree-huggers pissed me off, a bully always pissed me off more, and that kid had passed from loudmouth right into bully territory. You punch in your weight class. No one with any pride wants to see a puppy get kicked.

I was discretely stretching my shoulder muscles to get them primed for a quick one-two when the door opened. She strode in head-smart and street-sharp, street clothes hanging loosely but grabbing spots nonetheless. She plopped down beside me with all of the grace of a forty-five-year-old rail worker, but still, the eyes were on her.

"Fucking sausage party. Ain't it?" she said as the seat squeaked.

"Dollar-senses tingling, Jen?"

"I'm off the clock," she said, sitting a cold hand on my arm.

"How was tonight?"

"A bunch of no-tip dickheads cumming in their pants."

"Huh. My day felt about the same," I said.

I'm guessing she sensed how dead I felt through my arm, because her hand moved away to wave to the bartender. A polite quiet seemed to fall over the bar at her presence, but maybe it was just an excuse. None of these kids seemed ready for anything tough, so they probably would have taken the ice cream man as a good excuse. I tipped a finger to the bartender for another drink and made my way to the bathroom.

I held my dick feeling a bit let down by the actions of the night. What was going on with the world when so many chances were left on the bar? Why was Jenny there? The light flickered and a spider danced in the globe above.

"So, how'd you know I was here?" I asked as I

sat on the stool.

"You didn't come to see me, so where else would you be?" Jen asked.

"Shit, am I that predictable?"

"Like Big Ben, darlin'."

I sipped at my scotch, not liking myself in particular. I mean, shit, was I as bad as old Gen X over there? I thought I was doing interesting things. Maybe I was turning into those old, routine fucks at the old fuck side of the bar.

I woke up in a mood that would bend nails, my pillow was too hot and the sheets too cold and my hands felt like they were full of blended gelatin. I put my cup of hot water with a teabag that had been in my cupboard since Clinton played sax on the little table next to the window, and stuffed an envelope with enough cash to keep the landlord off of my back for a little while. Rain pattered against the window and trickled in slow where the frame met the wall, another gloomy day on this shitty spit of land.

The rain fell cold and breezy in that way that, no matter how you handled your umbrella, the

cuffs of your pants were going to be dripping before you reached the bottom of the stairs. Torn up papers and soda bottles and cigarette butts floated and drowned in the puddles lining uneven sidewalks. Traffic aimed for the pools of grime on the streets, timing their waves to capsize you. I pulled the crushed remnants of a pack of cigarettes from a pocket, and found a fresh pack of a brand I don't smoke in the other. Must've been a good night. Fuck if I remembered.

The first drag went down harsh and hearkened a wave of woozy that a new blend of heavy chemicals tends to do. The edge of my long coat fluttered around the ember in a worrying way and a slow seep of moisture pointed out a crack in my boot that had gone unnoticed until then. Our block on Pacific was horrid-recognition quiet in a way that made me think even the junkies in the flop-house across the street had taken the day off dying.

George was quiet, with a grey over his deep-in-thought face that made me keep my mouth shut as I grabbed a tea and burger and a normal bottle of water, instead of another can of bird vomit like

the day before. It actually wasn't bad, but I try to keep my vomit ingestion to once a week. A haze of static ran over his show from back home due to the storm, satellite was still cheaper than cable on the island. Lucky for me I didn't have to deal with either.

A note fluttered in the wind, wedged into the space between the door and jamb, and I had to move the burger from the key-hand to my teeth to grab it as I opened up. A slow drip was coming from somewhere in the drop ceiling, settling on that discolored patch like it did every time it rained.

A pair of girls from Ventnor popped in just as I settled down to read, the tired bags of those that partied too young hanging under their eyes—eyes redolent of the cult-like enthusiasm of recent membership to 'insert chemical of choice' anonymous. They giggled like kids, which they weren't too far from, but the crow's feet and little sags of flesh showed a rough time passed. I took a sip of tea, stretched my back, and set the mask firmly in place.

They weren't particularly terrible per se, just

the usual bubbles of the broken cheerleader, as so many of those types end up after the glamor of high school ends. I checked their IDs, because you can never be too careful there, whether for age or if they pass off bad bills. Everything checked out, they each asked for the first initial of the other on their wrist, a tragically typical idea that had gestated somewhere deep in the bowels of the internet, and had them grab a seat. I drew it small enough to make a newspaper typesetter blush, because that was clear and I saw the little, inept dance of the damned as they saw how 'cute' a typical letter form could be.

"Can it be... thinner?"

I saw this one coming. "It can be but," I rolled up my sleeve to one of my early career attempts at 'breaking the form' when I was an idiot and thought that that could be done, "this used to say 'still'. It doesn't say shit now. I just have to give that warning."

Problem one turned toward problem two and said "Chelsea has something that small and it looks fine."

"How long has Chelsea had hers for?" I asked,

her face looking like I had broken some sacred fourth wall at the intrusion.

"She's had it a while."

"Okay, so, how long? Because the blurring happens over time."

"Oh, she's had it seven months, so it'll be fine."

Oh, the glamored eyes of youth.

"Okie doke," I shrugged it off. They'd made enough shit choices to know better. If they wanted to make another, it was on them. Plus, it was a rainy day. Don't fuck around with the smooth of a rainy day.

I burned the stencils, and let them choose who would go first, which was a nearly insurmountable mountain. Of course, they both had to sit next to each other for emotional support, because, you know, people haven't been performing this rite without a helping hand for a few thousand years. I brought the needle in close on problem one, her jitterbug nerves from too many years on the spike making her skin shake like a little dog that had been kicked.

"I don't know," problem one said, pulling

her wrist right out of my grip an eighth of an inch from contact.

"You gotta let me know—" I said.

"You've got this, bitch," problem two cut in.

"Okay, okay, okay."

Her arm laid back on the armrest, shivering in a way that made me feel it in my feet through the stem of the armrest. I aimed the tight, little three—little wider than a hair width—and stretched the little gap between the fingers of my other hand.

"Shit!" she screamed, flexing her fist and twisting away.

I was lucky to have so many years in because, holding my breath as I wiped, I had pulled the needle away just in time. "You really need to hold still, or at least tell me if you're gonna move."

"I can't help it. It hurts!"

I didn't bother to bring up the fact that I had in fact helped it to end up with most of my body covered. I'm sure that there would have just been some other excuse, or a creepy attempt to be cute. I gripped tighter, pinning her wrist firmly to the armrest, locking every muscle I had free like a vise.

"Are you ready?" I asked.

"Just go ahead, she's fine," problem two said.

"Are you ready?" I asked again, focusing on the horror in my midst.

"Yeah, of course I am."

I focused every fiber of my being on keeping that writhing mass of junkie undulation under control; blocking the little, dumb noises from my ears; predicting the unpredictable jerks and shudders and squirms, you'd be amazed how many can be done in such a short time; and thirty seconds later we were done. I prayed to the vacant void that surely waited above my head and wiped the skin down with green soap. Every calligraphic shift was there, every serif a perfect width. The tattoo gods had shined down upon me. I had done what I had had to do against the unappreciative, over-expecting monster of the greater masses. A glob of A&D on the skin, a meat-packer taped over it, and she was all set.

"He didn't need to hold me so rough," problem one said to two, as they switched seats.

Problem two was easier and harder than problem one, but I had luckily stopped giving a shit about their feelings by then and focused solely

on the ends. The moans and lamentations went unheard, in a way that their privileged souls had never experienced before—I'm not your dad, and honestly don't give a shit about your feelings. The whims once again aligned and a dull, tiny letter, whose life would last all of a measly year if it was lucky, came out as clear and smooth as if it were sitting on a screen. I waited for that moment of 'um, we wanted the opposite letters,' but once again, the world decided not to batter me into its flesh. It was all coming up roses.

Wrapped up and done, they did the dance of telling each other how much they preferred the other's tattoo, before heading directly for the door. I had come to expect a lack of tips, as they had become an endangered species in recent years. I was already dead-eying their backs when problem two turned at the knob.

"Oh, I almost forgot to give you this," she said, reaching into her purse.

Well, wasn't I an asshole.

She pulled a folded bill out of her purse, the edge showing at the palm of her hand, and slid it over into my palm like we were doing a deal. Old

74

habits die hard.

"Thank you very much,", I said. "I appreciate it."

A 'bye' came somewhere through their rapid-fire back and forth between the two of them, and they were gone. The wind turned, rain spattered against the window, the neon illuminating beads of rain in garish colors, and I opened my palm. A five-dollar bill sat there, brown-stained in the corner with a tear down the center.

It was near seven before another foot fell through our door. They came in with every stereotype that reality television had trained us to expect—the gravity-defying puff of hair, the spray-on tan, the thoughtless fashion that was nothing but a copy loop that no one could pinpoint the origins of, the muscles doing nothing, brains doing even less. They flipped through the flash racks on the wall, laughing a mindless, judgment-with-no-backing 'yo cuz' with a point at every new page. Even without the stumbling bumbling, I could smell the energy drink cocktails mixing with their cheap cologne from the counter.

"Look at this bullshit," the meathead said to

his little, tan lackey, slapping the flash rack shut.

"Cazzo," the little one said.

Tiny actually had one of those 'American by birth, Italian by da' grace of God' shirts on, and the hair raised on my arms.

"Yo cuz, I wanna getta horn on my, my, arm chest. How much is you gonna charge?" The big, drunk, mindless pile with his Philly/New York/Wherever accent spilled.

"Alright bud," I said. "Why don't you come back tomorrow and we can do that no problem."

"Why the fuck would I come back tomrrow?" he slurred.

"Hey cuz, my kid is just tryina get some work done," Tiny said.

"I think your guy might have had enough fun."

The monster's face got real ready then, trying to look as scary as he could. "Jus' put a fuckin' horn on me, kid."

The problem is, you can't control anatomy. If their face gets red, that's all the blood they've got; their arms are already all vein so they think that'll trick you but there's nothing working them when the blood's all heading upward. A cool fell over me

and the mask dropped away.

"You've had enough. Go back to your fuckin' hotel if you want to get there on your own," I said.

I don't know if he was sentient enough to know that he was on the losing side, or if he was just having the outburst of a spoiled brat. "Fuck this place!" he said, pulling over the tall-backed chair next to him.

"You want to go now," I said.

"Let's go," Tiny said.

"No, fuck this stronzo," the big one said.

He took a step toward the counter, expecting me to step back. I did the opposite, coming around the counter barehanded. I wasn't too worried. Hesitation fluttered across his eyes that someone wasn't dead-scared. I saw his hands flex twice without any confidence.

"Alright kid, it's time to go," I said, taking another step toward him. He was about my height, but a good foot wider.

He looked over to his friend, who was damned near at the door. His right hand pulled tight, his bicep tightened, and he threw a hay-maker Rocky would have been proud of. In the damned near

thirty minutes I had before his fist got near me, I put my forearm against his, flexed my open hand, and stepped back slightly. His own force hit him; the base of my palm struck his jaw, his fist slid right past me, and he tumbled in a ball at my feet.

"Get this piece of shit out of my shop," I said to Tiny, who was already scurrying over to that beast.

I waited until the little one had dragged his friend out of the shop before I moved. I saw him trying to wake his buddy out in the rain of a dying sun while I clicked the lock on the door. His fake tan shifted in the deluge of rain as he lay on his back.

I pulled the blinds and headed for a piss. My hands shook like those junkie girls, I was getting too fucking old. A dull thud on the door met my ears as I closed the bathroom door.

I hit a piss, wondering where the day had gone, wondering how I had put myself into this place. I swear, I was a nice kid. Where had I fucked up so bad?

A sign above the toilet said, 'LIGHT IS MO-TION ACTIVATED', and my eyes locked on it.

BETTER LIVING
THROUGH BLOODSHED

At some point in the years that I had been there, I had become fixed on the thought that if you switched the first two letters of *motion activated*, it would describe me pretty well. A little sign could just hang above me perpetually saying, 'Action Motivated'. That was the only way that I ever felt alive. Maybe it wasn't such a fuck up after all to be here. Maybe I was just aging out.

With me well and truly done for the day, I wrote out my cash drop, the trash good to wait another day, and the little folded note from when I'd opened caught my attention. Ink had bled through the yellow paper a bit from the rain, and the one edge was a sloppy tear from a notebook. I unfolded the sheet and pressed it flat against the counter. In one line of block lettering was written the inscription. 'KEEP YOUR EYES OPEN'

If I said this was the first time I had gotten a note of some junked-up ravings, I'd be lying. Crack and meth and dope do some strange things to the human mind, and they tended to give these sad souls the impression that their delusions were the only real truth; that they just had to warn as many

people as often as possible about the coming destruction; that they were the benefactors of some strange mystical glimpse beyond the veil. 'THE POLICE ARE BUGGING YOU', 'ARCTIC AVE IS THE GATEWAY TO HELL', 'THE ILLUMINATI TRANSMITS THROUGH CHICKEN NUGGETS', slipped into palms, or under doors, or into mail slots. I'd seen them all.

So, it was with little hesitation that I crumpled the note, tossed it into the trash beside the thermofax, and put on my jacket in an attempt to somehow turn this shit-show day around. The rain had turned into a lazy mist from the heavens, swirling in a deranged dance around the streetlights. A puddle of puke sat where that big pile of slow must have woken up, and I hoped the rain would pick up before morning to wash it away. For the time being, I would enjoy the way the mist danced across my face in the breeze, breathing a little more life into me, care of the night.

Some sad-sack sat on the corner, a block from Caesar's, rainwater slipping over the toes of his wingtips in the gutter, head in his hands. "Lost it all," he said. "Lost it all. Whatam I gonna do?"

BETTER LIVING
THROUGH BLOODSHED

It had been a nice suit once, before all of the grime and sadness had stained it up. His hand gripped a pile of receipts for a wagered house, car, and a few more, and a cup at his side still held the remnants of a watered-down cocktail that they give to the losers so they won't hold a grudge.

"What the hell am I gonna do?" he slurred, those hopeless eyes, drunk enough that they couldn't focus on me, staring up. "Where am I gonna go?"

"Walk across the beach and keep walkin', pal."

They might find his body in the morning, a big dive off a parking garage, or washed up on shore, or stabbed to death behind a motel, or they might not. It didn't much matter to me either way. He was all chewed up for keeps, and the last thing the city needed was another soul-broke charity case. We had enough of them local.

Mary's windows were all dark—she'd been asleep for hours—a big house from a better time in Atlantic City. Seagull and starfish wind chimes tinkled above the door, and a rotten tree branch from the neighbor's groaned overhead. I took twenty fifties out of my pocket and slid them through the

mail slot, no note, no nothing. Mary deserved a good morning without strings attached.

The headlights of a jitney flared light across a couple of bums around a trashcan fire in the abandoned, fenced-in parking lot next to Dead Heat. I finished my smoke and watched them pass a bottle in a paper bag. This wasn't some after-school special. They didn't look at you with 'save the children' eyes. They were having a grand old time in the chilled mist, each getting sauced with someone who knew them, someone who understood.

"Hey," I shouted over their tubercular laughter.

Their faces turned hesitant, but street ready. I waved over and the more fit looking of the two came over, which doesn't say much of the other.

"Either of you fellas need a smoke?" I asked when he reached the other side of the fence. A little sad cavity had opened up in my chest at some point, and I needed to close it up.

"Not me," he said through a stained, white beard, "but Danny could." He took a swig from the bottle.

"What're you drinkin'?" I asked as I pulled out

my pack.

He slid a bottle of that fruit-flavored, sugar rot-gut that might be cheap but it costs a hell of a lot on your kidneys.

"Jesus," I said and dug my hand back into my pocket. "Get something that's gonna kill you with a bit more fun." I slipped him a twenty with a couple of smokes.

"Thanks, pal."

"You kids stay safe."

I might be an asshole in a lot of ways, but I've got my own set of morals. Bums weren't the rubes at the tables throwing their money away, or shoobies to hustle that were just coming to shit all over the city anyway, or folks in the game that knew what they were getting into from the start. More times than not, they were just poor fucks that got dealt the shitty hand that fate was trying to deal to all of us.

One of Tommy's bouncers hugged the doorway of Ocean View, his cheap sharkskin suit spotted black from rain; as dumb as he was, he clocked me as I entered Dead Heat. If my timing was right, this should go smooth as silk. I nodded at Stimey

as I came in, and there must have been something to my look because he just slid my drink over without a fight. The first one went down with only a little burn in my empty gut, and I slipped him a twenty when he handed me another. "Thanks, brother," I said and headed for the back door.

Piss alley smelled a little fresher from the rain and an empty room greeted me as I passed over into Ocean View. Galaxy looked up with a glimmer of hope from where she sat on the stage and quickly went back to her biology book. She only had another semester to go after her summer courses.

I walked up and passed a five into her hand, as I preferred to do; you don't pass your tip between the tits of a waiter, why do it at a club? It must have been a stone-dead night because even the DJ was on autopilot, some random compilation of club hits playing in full while he drowsed behind the booth. I grabbed a seat at the little bar, its only purpose to give out ice and glasses, closest to the changing room.

It might have been one song or two, I couldn't tell with those shitty Euro-hits, before Jen came

out. She was in more street-ready clothes than usual, as opposed to the quick-change stuff that she usually wore before our second shift, which boded poorly. She gave me a less-than-overjoyed look, which boded even worse.

"Hmm," she said as I sidled up to her walking past.

"Any work tonight?"

"So, now you want to see me, Phil?"

Shit.

"When have I ever not wanted to?" I put a hand on her arm, which was coldly pulled away.

Double-shit.

"After last night, I didn't expect to see you any time soon."

What the hell did I do?

"Don't be so harsh," I bluffed.

"You spend all night getting cuddly at the bar, buy me flowers from that kid on the corner, walk me all the way home, and what?" She turned some frozen-granite eyes on me. "You give some fall-over bow and stumble off?"

Oh shit. Thank fuck. That's nothing.

"Who would I be if I didn't walk a lady home?"

That didn't get me anywhere.

"Well, it's a lovely night, and you look like you could use one," I said, "so how about a drink?"

The granite was going a bit wobbly, but I still had some work to do.

"No mixed signals," I said. "Scouts honor."

"You were never a scout."

The Pub was steady, because The Pub was always steady. The stools along the first side of the bar were all taken, photos of boxers, and Irish movie stars, and framed newspaper clippings lining the wall at their backs. At the far side, near the entrance to the backyard, I spotted a pair of open stools. They weren't touching, but it wouldn't be too hard to talk folks into sliding over for a pretty girl like Jen. Always better than having to sit in the dining room, anyway.

I ordered a round for us, and one for the spider-veined noses that had moved for us as we sat down. You never want to owe anyone for anything in this town. Jen ordered a cheap drink for her first, which she always did and it always annoyed me; as though I would think there was some re-

ciprocal contract for a good drink. I pantomimed that I was going to go smoke and motioned to the bartender as I passed by, telling him the drink that Jen actually wanted, as opposed to what she had ordered, on my way.

The boardwalk loomed dead up the ramp at my right as I smoked, the Ferris wheel slowly doing its circuit without a soul to enjoy it, and the side street dark from shot-out street lights to my left. The parking lot was devoid of anything interesting, which was a shame because you could occasionally find some very interesting interactions occurring. I stubbed out my cigarette, as a seagull sang starvation, and passed through the heavy pair of doors.

My legs had that dumb heaviness of exhaustion as I crossed those revelry backs, and I tried as I could try to give them some more life. Jenny was chatting up the livers-of-the-damned as I got back to my seat, always the money maker, and she had the twinkle in her eye that told me that she had gotten the better drink. If she knew that I had gotten it for her, that was okay, if she thought that she had gotten it on her own card of looks and charm, all the better.

Zachary Von Houser

Henchey locked in on me before I even sat down, and his skeletal, shitty grin was on me as I took my first sip. He had been a shitty cop, the type that would smash a kid's head against the edge of his car door as he put him into the back seat; which I knew because he had smashed my head against the edge of his door more times than I could count when I was a kid. The thing was, I wasn't a kid anymore, he wasn't a scary giant anymore, and his malevolent smile showed more fear than anything in bigger eyes. I saw the shiver of his elbows through his uniform as he lifted himself from the stool and made his way over.

"O'Niell, O'Niell, whatever will we do with you," he asked, the last dregs of a stout in his glass and whiskey-shine in his eyes.

"I'm guessing nothing, because I'm not twelve anymore."

There was a twitch in his left eye. "You should learn to respect the brotherhood."

"I think I might..." I said. "If you dickheads did anything worth respecting."

The drunks nearest to us dropped the tone of their conversation a little, glances barely peeking

over at us in that glassy way.

His eyes went mean, in that drunk cop way, and he finished the foam and slop at the bottom of his glass. "You've always been a little prick, O'Niell." He swayed at my side. "You're gonna learn your place, O'Niell. You're gonna," hiccup, "learn your place."

Jen looked over at me, a nervousness to her expression that made my blood boil for some reason.

"Not before you do. I'm not a kid anymore and can handle myself." He turned to Jen, his shitty mustache shivering with joy and drunkenness,

"Did this little prick ever tell you about how scared he got when I booked him?"

My heart beat heavy, my head swam. "Like I said, I'm not a kid anymore, sweetheart."

"Yeah, yeah. You tough guys always think you're above the law if you don't learn early enough. You'll see just how small you are when the cuffs go on." He splashed some sad dregs on Jenny's top.

She wasn't enjoying herself, and at the moment neither was I.

"Hopefully not before you're in the dirt, Henchey." I felt my stomach tighten.

"That's a threat on an officer, kid."

"Okay, okay," I said, playing a bit more drunk and motioning him in. When his ear was right next to mine, I whispered, "When you're falling into that hole, you're gonna look up at me."

"I'll let it slide," he said with a lizard's sneer, but I could see the lack of confidence growing. "You're gonna dig your own grave."

He stumbled back to his seat. I saw his ribs spread with a blade, I saw the back of his skull crumble under a bat, I saw his knees go the wrong way under the weight of a crowbar. I looked at Jen, and she had this look of sympathy that I couldn't bear. He didn't know the violence that he could be forced to endure, he didn't know the brutality of the world. More than anything, he didn't know the grudge I could hold.

I would have usually just let that slide. You don't casually go against John Law in the city, especially with so little reason. Now, here I was, a public grudge against one of the most crooked pricks to wear a badge, and that's saying a lot. Why had I

forced that hand into a situation that I definitely couldn't control?

"I'm getting a bit tired," I said to Jen as Henchey sat down, indulging in only the vaguest of lies. I could already feel my arms going numb with exhaustion. I wondered how much sleep I had gotten. Henchey smirked at me and I put a hundred on the bar.

Why was I being so defensive? Why was I being so protective? Was I getting tipsy or was I letting things get complicated?

He turned toward us, with his kid-killer teeth and his shoot-to-kill mustache, as we passed, and it took everything I had not to hit him. You really need to calculate first hits if you're going to make it far. Hold a grudge for long enough that the DA can't possibly hold a case.

A cab was waiting out front as we passed through the second door. I gave a wave so that he wouldn't think that we were robbing him, and opened the door. Jen went around the door and stopped. This would have been the perfect moment for some fairytale kiss, the moon big and bold above us, the red neon shining across the side

of her face, the rain drumming in the puddles of the big parking lot; but this wasn't some fairytale, and the cold-badness of the world usually prevails. So, I gave her a little smile through the window and watched the cab pull away. I considered going back in, I'm not too proud to say, grabbing the closest bottle or glass, and putting Henchey on desk work for the rest of his shit career, but that's how you get popped. Worse, I'm sure a rat like that would just find a more lucrative way to be crooked from that view.

I took a deep breath of cooler heads prevailing and strolled toward Pacific. The wind picked up off of the ocean, the rain tumbling against the back of my neck, and I heard a shout from the Pic. I was about halfway to Pacific, so the view was a bit far for me. A couple was standing in front of the little shed-cum-restaurant but nothing serious seemed to be going on. That's the problem with ocean breezes, they've been free too long, so the second they hit the civilized world they don't know how to act.

"O'Niell!" The shout was a little to the side of my view. I turned toward the pub, my eyes squint-

ing against the barrage of rain, where Henchey was standing at the door. From that distance, his uniform shrinking into his body from the rain, he looked even smaller, and I almost, almost, felt a little sorry.

"What?" I shouted.

"It's about that time."

I could blame the rain, or the confusion about what he was talking about, or the drinks, but when it comes down to it, I hadn't been at my best game all damned day. So, when the footsteps from behind me came, and the alarm bells should have been screaming, I was just standing there getting soaked like so many nameless rubes until the lights went out.

When I started to come to, it didn't smell like piss and sweat, and the whiskey that I could smell wasn't the sour-mash rot of a cop's budget, so I wasn't locked up. My face stung, my mouth tasted like copper, and from the heavy beat of it, my heart felt like it had been transplanted into the back of my skull. I started to crack my eyes and the light was a swirling toilet. I closed them again

to keep my drinks down, and the rustling leaves of conversation tried to force itself in between the thud-thud in my skull.

I felt my head swung sharp to the side by some force besides my own, but my face felt like that dead numb that surrounds a bad break in a bone. Strong cologne stung my nose, my head shook back and forth with a scary sloshing from somewhere deep. My arm jittered as I brought it to my face and, although I could feel my face, my face couldn't feel my fingers.

"Wake up, you jamoke." A fat finger lifted my eyelid, and the rough lumps of a misshapen face came in and out of focus. "I think he's bullshittin', Mister Giordano. You want me to break a finger to check?"

"I'm not bullshittin' anything," I said, but from the confused grumbling I'm guessing it came out more like 'Uhna bullshtin anthin."

"Speak up, kid," the voice said, and a sharp sting in my already stinging face brought me closer to the world.

"Fuck!" The tip of a blade pulled back from under my eye, as my head pulled back from the fat

94

hand holding the handle still. "Some hospitality."

My head shot to the side, and I felt the palm a little more distinctly this time. "Show some respect, ya little prick."

"Pauly, Pauly, Pauly. A cordial notion doesn't cost a thing," an even voice said from somewhere beyond the plump shoulders. I could tell the words were tumbling around in his skull like the whiskey was in my gut.

"He's saying, quit being a dickhead." The hand pulled back again as I said it, but thought better in case I happened to be telling the truth, which I felt like I didn't have the concentrative abilities to stop doing.

"Very succinct, Mister O'Niell. A thing very lacking in these over-spoken times."

Pauly stepped aside, and for the first time his fat wasn't blocking most of my view. Everything was still a bit air-over-a-hot-street, but I had gained enough wherewithal after the little poke to know that I wasn't upside down. It wasn't a huge room, there weren't more than a handful of those on the whole island for private use, but the two walls of window, with their sweeping view a handful of sto-

ries high, overlooked downbeach to one side and the ocean to the other. So, pretty much, ocean, ocean, and a little strip of boardwalk, and far off Ventnor. It was still the dead of night, I hadn't been unconscious for that long, that would have been dangerous, but the fact that it was utterly black, short of the little strip of light in the corner, oriented me. The room had an old-school chic that screamed of personal decorator; the books on the shelves that lined one wall to my side were all color-coordinated collections without a wrinkle in the spines; The desk was one of those big, walnut things, but I could see the little strips of tape that stopped scuffing toward the bottom of the legs, with an over-sized, over-red chair behind it; I couldn't tell what was behind me, because the eye in the back of my head was swollen shut.

The man strolling forward from behind the desk wasn't big, but he wasn't small and he wasn't in terrible shape. He had that rectangle face and Palminteri hairline that is so unfortunate with the dagos. A nice suit cut in to strong shoulders, and stronger-than-fat arms that flexed under an expensive suit as he lit a cigar; it was one of those dinky,

little things that people smoke when they want you to know that they smoke but don't really want to smoke. I always hated cigars, they just stink of cat piss. As he got closer, a nicer cologne started to seep into that cheap shit that Pauly wore to block out the rank sweat.

"Rise up on my spokes, but don't complain when you're thrown back down," Giordano said as he crouched down. Apparently, I was sitting. "It's surprising, the whims of fate, Mister O'Niell."

"You're telling me."

"Again, the brevity. You know, the problem is, brevity breeds laziness. The occasional, brief point makes me think, 'this is a man of business. This is a man who knows how to get things done.' Unfortunately, after a continual assault, like most assaults, the impact is lost and you eventually see the faults. I see a great fault here, Mister O'Niell. Do you know what that is?"

"I couldn't possibly," I placated.

"Much better," he said and puffed a stream of smoke right under my nose. "A soldier ant is an interesting thing. It spends its whole life defending its nest, killing, destroying, procreating. It lives,

what it considers to be a warrior's life. Again, its problem is its perspective. In its world," he said and put his hand on mine, which I found was on the wooden arm of a chair, "it is the unstoppable force of some greater good." He squeezed my hand, his palm over-soft. "The fault is a level of hierarchy. In its little, little mind, the universe ends within the confines of its sad, little world. Have you ever thought like an ant, Mister O'Niell?"

"I can't say that I have."

"So, an ant might go into a den of centipedes and, having never been able to see the back of itself, or itself in general, it might think 'well, this seems like me, they act like me, they kill like me." The seconds ticked in that expensive grandfather clock. I knew that one of us had to talk, and it wouldn't be him. "Okay."

He looked disappointed, dad-to-a-teenager disappointed. "Why did you take my money, O'Niell?"

I didn't expect that level of direct action. "What money?" was the only thing that I could respond.

His brow furrowed, and he got lost in some

spot on the carpet between us. "From what I can tell, you're not a stupid man, and I'm very rarely wrong in my judgment." He took a step closer, his shoes only a foot or so from mine, his hand dancing in the black suit jacket. "So, I'll presume that you misheard, and the what in your question was one of having not heard. My money, O'Niell. Why did you take my money?"

The hand was either moving around an implement of injury or evidence, a hand wouldn't be that animated attached to such a calm demeanor otherwise. Neither of those options left me with the upper hand, the spins still too strong to give me a good chance in a fight, my head too loopy to argue my way out of a piece against me. She sells sea shells and all. What? Focus. Okay, so either way, the jig was up and the only way out was the straight and narrow. Honesty is always a dangerous gambit in situations of such potential harm, but it can also put people off balance. They expect you to bullshit all the way to the bottom of the bay with a chain around your neck.

"Seemed like the guy didn't have much use for it anymore," I said, looking Giordano dead in the

eye. A tough maneuver when you feel blood running below your own.

"Hmm," he turned toward the unused bookshelf. "You're local, but I don't think you're dumb enough to rob a man you killed, and I doubt that, even if you had, you'd be able to get Nicky into a position to put two into the top of his skull while he was on his knees."

He looked over at me, but I didn't know what face he was looking for, so I just did the dumb one that seemed to be hovering across my muscles.

"So, that tells me you only robbed the dead," the disgust seemed to be leaking from between his lips, "and me by proxy. I don't care for grave robbers, Mister O'Niell." His hand stopped dead in his pocket, the bulge telling me that a fist was gripping something. "But you didn't call the authorities. Whether from fear, which seems unlikely, or from a general distaste for them," it was like a bridge gapped our locked eyes, "I have less trouble respecting a man that leaves things to be settled in family."

"Never have gotten along with Johnny Law," I said, with something thick choking up the top of

my throat.

"Nor have I, Mister O'Niell." His hand slowly emerged from his pocket, and I felt the cheek closest to his tighten in anticipation, whether hammer, blade, or bullet.

A knot of cash wrapped in a rubber band, which I immediately recognized, emerged from his pocket. My socks suddenly felt a lot lighter.

"Two-thousand five-hundred dollars," he said, twirling the knot in between thumb and forefinger. "Out of six thousand."

"Five and some change."

"Pardon?"

"I pulled five and some change from your boy."

"Your lack of ambition is of no concern to me," he said. "There was six thousand dollars on Nicky at the time of his untimely demise. If you couldn't be bothered to collect the rest, I believe that has some bearing on your character and not the whims of fate."

He wasn't wrong, I did leave some bills blowing in the wind when I thought it was all chump change.

"So, as I was saying, out of six thousand, here is an even two-thousand five-hundred dollars."

"What about the other one?" I asked.

"The other what, Mister O'Niell?"

"The other knot."

"That was all of the money on your person."

"Then talk to your man. I'd guess that—"

"My nephew."

"Hmm?"

"You would guess about my nephew. Now, what is it that you would guess about my nephew?" His pupils were a couple of dark graves seen from the wrong side of the hole.

"I would guess that he might know if he saw me drop some cash in the parking lot."

"He saw no such thing, I can assure you." He gestured for me to stand. The world shivered under my feet, and I had to keep a firm flex on my knees to keep me upright. Everything pumped in my eyes like I did too many whip-its. The slop in my guts defied gravity and I felt it fighting its way up my esophagus.

"I'm sure that you'll be bringing me the rest of my money in a very timely manner, Mister

O'Niell."

"Not a problem," I said, Giordano grabbing my hand.

"That's not a concern of mine."

Pauly saw my way down the elevator. A clump of crap in the corner of his eye, and a stain on the collar of his shirt divided my attention. He was trying his best to give the scary-guy to me, but I just wasn't buying, and I couldn't help but notice the way that him noticing I didn't buy it bulged a vein on the side of his head. At his weight, he should really look out for such things. He kept rubbing his hand across the butt of the piece in his waistband through his jacket (a real cheap piece of shit), as though I couldn't take it from him before he could pull it. Hell, in my state, maybe I couldn't. Either way, I wouldn't be testing the theory if I could help it.

We passed through an opulently decorated lobby that I had never seen before and, as we crossed the threshold, I felt a foot smaller than mine kick me onto the wooden slats of the walkway down to the street. I turned back, but not before Pauly

had shut the door behind him with a smirk. Those fat folds receded into the glare of the glass and I picked myself up off the splintery boards.

The sun was rising on the ocean, but not high enough to kill the twilight of the big buildings. What a dumb old way the sun worked, sunrise here when it's still dark at the far end of the time-zone. What happened to the kids that lived down the street in opposite time zones? How did they coordinate when to hang out? My feet thumped on sand burrs and chip bags. Whose timezone prevailed? I mean, when you can barely come to a consensus on the little world of grade-school politics, who decides who wins on loftier matters? Like... time zones. What? Alright, I was on Pacific. I was headed downbeach. How far had I come? 'Where was I', wasn't really a question, because after a few blocks, you would always know where you were in Atlantic City. I hit Georgia and cut a right.

I've always hated a cop bar, even if it was a cop/firefighter bar, but it was close by and I needed a drink. My distaste for cops would always outweigh my appreciation for firefighters. Especially on that morning. I hadn't had a chance to see how

BETTER LIVING
THROUGH BLOODSHED

Henchey was tied into this, but I doubted that that dumb fuck had just fallen into such luck to see me get hit, especially considering his lack of retribution when I had talked shit in front of his bar cronies.

I walked in, and Atlantic City's best and brightest in blue looked over like I had just set their moms on fire, the incomprehensible thought that someone outside their fold would dare to encroach on such a sacred right left them dumbfounded. How would they be able to freely discuss the acts of violence that they perpetrated on the general public now? I sure was a real son of a bitch.

My scotch tasted like water with a little fireplace ash in it, if the rocks weren't from a urinal they should really get their lines checked. Some Irish tune was playing on the jukebox, but some polished shit from the nineties, not anything from a time worth listening to. Half of the assholes in there were smoking cigars that smelled like the seat of a dead bum's pants, and the ones that weren't were yammering without a breath until I wished those dog turd cigars were mandatory if you wanted a badge. The eye-balling hadn't eased up with

me taking a seat at the far, vacant end of the bar, and I wondered how there could be such a sheer volume of dickhead on the force with so little in those cheap pants. I finished my drink and made for the bathroom.

Police patches from all fifty lined the walls below the crown molding, with a few from far-off lands peppered in; I guess that brotherhood passes on to places that they call subhuman on a daily basis. Ashtrays between the splattered urinals overflowed with cigar butts, and a few tiny baggies that I couldn't possibly assume the provenance of, and a long trail of toilet paper ran clear from one to the stalls to the bathroom door. After taking a piss and getting a look in the mirror, the looks that I had gotten at the door made a bit more sense. Brown parking lot water stained a puddle from the collar down one side of my shirt, with a disturbingly vivid darkening around the edge; a line of flaky, dried blood ran from a pinpoint under my eye amid a rough splotch where my face had hit asphalt; from somewhere in the back, my collar blotched forward rusty-red, like a cloth tarp over the beaches of Normandy.

106

BETTER LIVING
THROUGH BLOODSHED

Well, it takes all types to make the world move. If they actually saw when shit got interesting on a daily basis, they wouldn't be too shocked to see someone in this state. Why didn't cops only get paid when they were working? Plenty of other service workers in the world worked that way. If you weren't doing one type of work, then you found something else to keep busy, otherwise you didn't get paid. Why was it that I was paying the check for these assholes to just stroll around for eighty percent of their shift doing fuck all? Shit. How long had I been in here thinking this?

I splashed cold water on my face, passively rinsing the blood from my cheek. Focus Phil. This is no time for your head to be pumping high-octane nonsense. I went in close on the snot-flicked mirror, pulling my lower eyelids down, staring at my pupils. I looked at my eyes, stared up at the reflection of the fluorescent bulbs, back at my eyes. The slow response of dilation wasn't a good sign. I considered taking off my shirt to rinse the blood from the collar, but saw the madness that I was happily marching toward. Another drink would clear it up, my brain felt like it was running on all

gears at the wrong timing and I needed to rein it in a bit. It was a battle of two beasts in the same body.

I ordered a pint and a shot, to prevent the confusion that I wanted silt-water and the ice from a mammoth's ass, and relaxed back into my seat. My shoulders ached from some tensing that I hadn't noticed I was doing, and the tingle of a thousand spiders danced over the back of my scalp. I took a sip from the pint and was pleasantly surprised to find four or five bubbles left in the glass. Service sure was shaping up. Some badge-off-gun-on dickhead wandered up as I was fighting down the fire of a whiskey far from the quality that I had ordered.

"I think you're in the wrong bar, kid."

I have a pretty good rule of thumb, which has served me well since long before I was legally able to enter a fine establishment such as this. If ever an asshole wanted me to walk out of a place, I might as well have needed a wheelchair. Nothing fucking doing. I had just as much right as any other asshole that was shat into this world.

"I'm just trying to have a drink, pal," I lit a cigarette to counteract the bum's pants.

108

BETTER LIVING
THROUGH BLOODSHED

"You should get moving along, before someone remembers how you acted last night."

I pinched my far leg hard enough the make a welt to keep my head straight. Huh. There were a few things that made this an interesting turn of events. Point one. Either sweetheart had enough rickets to call in Sarah McLachlan for a fundraiser, or he was pissed as a mule to the point where his knees were about to give out. Point two. There was either a serious sewing circle of cop drama, which was quite likely with how busy at work those kids usually were, or, if Henchey was involved, it went a bit farther than that mustachioed fuck. Either way, I knew that they would never do anything to disparage the name, and lawlessness, of their favorite city bar, and it would take more balls than any of them had to do real work in the light of day outside. The rest of them were all staring over, trying to do their tough guy faces and failing in the way that every cop has ever failed in the history of every cop. You just couldn't fake that look, and some proto-cop had made that bad call about how to look hard, and they had all followed it in the same way. I'm sure that even if they intended to kill you,

a cop couldn't do a sufficient semblance of a scary face while they did. Let's see how it would play.

"You do what you gotta sweetheart," I said, dead-faced, looking through those wandering glances into the wall on the other side of his head, "I'm sure you'll get a silver star for the eye you'll lose here." I lifted the shot glass by its base.

"Just keep it up tough guy," he said to me while looking at his little cluster of friends, "and see how far you get."

"I'll take those odds," I looked as bored as I could. "That's the funny thing, though."

"What's that?" He rubbed his brow, the wedding ring glinting slightly less than the stupid cop-brotherhood-bullshit ring on his pinky.

"Everyone knows where I work if I start any shit. Right?"

"You'd better believe it," he gave a smirk that made it so much sweeter.

"But my work never puts me into a dark alley with a person with a grudge." I lifted my pint from the bar. "How's that family of yours set in case something were to happen?"

The gray that his face went couldn't be hidden

by the red lighting, that beautiful classic that I hated for some reason in this setting. There was no guessing where this would go. I might have played my hand too strong, maybe just inside. Either way, I was overstepping very well set bounds for the second time in twenty-four hours. John Law only overlooked shit to a certain level, and then only if you weren't on the kill list, which I was certainly on now.

The condensation on the glass was getting slick in my hand, but you never take a drink when trouble is brewing. That's the oldest trick in the book. The base of a pint glass is orders of magnitude thicker than the sides of the glass so, when someone is getting smart and takes a sip of their pint, as they are often wont to do, if you punch the bottom of the glass, the base won't shatter but the sides will. Then, you have ringed them, as in you've sliced a hellish ring from the corners of the mouth up to the bridge of the nose, with plenty of beautiful, shattered glass in the eyes. Don't get ringed.

Old wobble-legs tried that fourth grade bullshit of jerking his shoulders forward like he was

going to hit me, which told me that he wasn't, in fact, going to hit me, and I could happily take a sip of my beer in front of him. The sun hit a point where the fake stained glass was lacking, and a sword edge of light illuminated the smoke hovering mid-bar. I'm guessing that he realized I wasn't terrified, I'd already stopped paying attention, more from whatever was going on in my mind than being tough, and I watched the interesting play of light as he broke it asunder.

What in the fuck was I doing in this place? I couldn't be forced there on the best of days, so what the shit kept my ass planted there then? I stood up and straightened my shirt, appearances still mattered, and slowly finished the pint. The eyes were distorted through the curve of the glass as I put it down. I wouldn't be forced out, but this was a certain level of purgatory that I would have to question my Catholic upbringing for forcing me to endure.

Luckily, Giordano's guys didn't give me too thorough of a search, and I reached for the torn edge of the label on the back of my Levi's for my emergency fund. I don't know what wobbles

thought I was going for, because his hand shot for the back of his own pants.

"Calm down, Wyatt Earp," I said, and slowly pulled out the little stack of folded twenties.

A line of mutters, and little more, met my wake as I passed the chubby, blue line at the bar and approached the blinding square at the door. I'd still left a twenty as a tip, hoping that the wrinkled mess behind the taps was there from sheer desperation. I'm not a monster.

The light outside felt like the sound of nails on a chalkboard somewhere deep in my brain. Something wasn't right, and I should probably go get it checked out. At least the sauce made it a bit more dull.

Even if Giordano's nephew hadn't run my one ankle for a roll, which I'm sure he had, it wouldn't be in the parking lot anymore. I had to get thirty-five hundred, and I had to get it quick.

After a couple of hours rest, the brittle light of blinds left open crashed down upon me on the couch. A rocky morning, in and out of sleep, had ended a half-hour earlier, but it was only once the

sun had risen just-so that its intrusive rays reached the point to drive me from my repose. Ripples of nausea had started in force about the time that I had laid down, and in their valleys I could sleep, but at the crest I rocked myself lightly to try and keep it down.

I sat up slow, like I told all of the kids that went green in my tattoo chair, creeping forward and only stopping when the floor started to reach for me. The world was a tread-bare rag of clarity wrinkling under my view. A glass of water helped as much as a glass of water has ever helped anyone not trapped at sea, and the handful of aspirin came back up as quick as they went down.

The three-quarter coat with a collar popped and scally cap hanging low gave me a bit of the anonymous comfort that my paranoia-riddled brain was craving. It's one thing to have that hangover fear of 'what did I do' pumping adrenaline through your post-blackout form, it's another to still have those vacant gaps, with recognizably terrible ideas peppered into what you did still grasp. I'd been through the latter before, but never quite to that extent. The limp drizzle of rain found its

way down my collar, and the cold wet shocked my brain into a state of focus that I didn't know was waning.

I skipped George's, knowing a microwaved sandwich would just come back up, and that my frazzled brain would only feel worse with the addition of caffeine, and pocketed another note that had been slid into our door. The swelling on the back of my skull had gone down, but I'd had enough concussions to recognize the fuzzy brain that accompanies one, and this one was a doozy. The hum of the neon stung my nerves in a certain way that harmonized with the hum already roaring through my brain as I clicked it on, and showed no signs of easing up on that front.

I put on my best salesman show, but no matter how well I sold, no one was biting. That's just the way that the tattoo gods want to look down upon you sometimes. Still, a little twinge of anxiety grew inch by inch with each umbrellaed figure that passed the plate-glass window beyond the shop's painted name, or came in just to kill time and actually meant it. Dead days mean something very different when you're in the red to someone

that no one should be in the red two. The problem is, sons of bitches like that are too easy to owe to and too hard to get out from under the thumb of.

About an hour before close, a familiar face came in, but not one that I was ever too keen to see. I'd heard his raspy, cigar laugh before he hit the door, but had hope that it was just a figment of my bruised brain. No such luck.

Angelo came in with a working girl on his arm. Not one of the ladies from out on Pacific, he needed someone presentable on the poker floor, but not much better. He came in facing her, his fat, drooping cheeks jiggling as he talked her ear off; but the smile dropped for just a second as he turned toward me and the empty shop.

"Finally... slowed down today, huh?" He gave a little nervous laugh at the end.

"Looks like it, boss," I said and slid back from the opening between the waiting room and the tattoo floor.

I'm guessing Angelo had been talking the place up all night as 'the most bumpin' shop in the city' or how 'wild' it would get in there, because his date for the night had a shocked look from the

116

banality of it all.

"You should have seen this place a few hours ago," he said, scratching his eczema arms with fat, over-sized baby fingers. "Packed with people just begging to get tats done."

He hadn't been in since last summer, so I had no idea where he was getting that information from.

"So busy they were askin' me to get to work." The wet laugh fell out of a little mouth squished in between ham cheeks. "All those guns goin', just like music. Guess Phil-boy here is just cleaning up after everyone. He's the new guy." He turned and smirked superiority at her, as though I was edging in on his lady.

"What's this... music? I thought you said it was like a club in here?" I could hear the crack scars in her throat.

"Oh Jesus, Phil." He waddled over to the stereo. "I leave this place for a couple of hours..."

He pulled my CD from the player, dropping it onto the rough shelf with a *shht* that made my eye twitch, and slipped a mix of last year's pop-nonsense in. The mix was courtesy of one of the shit-

heel summer workers that he brought back with him from Philly every year, promising fame and a flood of easy money, and producing fuck all. They all had dumb fucking tagging names that you had to learn, even though you knew they wouldn't make it two months; I think our current musical benefactor had been named Sguigs, or Bone-Eyes, or Terrence. Who knows? What I did know, as the aggressively mediocre bass line dragged itself along, was that if I ever saw him again, I was definitely going to punch him in the dick of this moment of agony.

"Well, hot stuff, how abouts we head up to my place?" The clogged arteries in his arm gestured toward the door in the back of the shop.

"You're place is here?"

"Upstairs. It's gorgeous."

It wasn't gorgeous; not that he would know if it had magically become so. The only person that had passed through that door in nine months had been his cousin-lackey-pillhead, Tommy, to straighten things up, keep the fridge stocked with the type of food that kept Angelo in that radial shape, and pass out after popping too many percs.

BETTER LIVING
THROUGH BLOODSHED

The heavy clank of the door locking behind them was followed by the sound of the stairs crying under such weight, and a forced giggle as they reached the top. I waited for the thud of equally terrible music blaring in Angelo's apartment to start, before I took the mix out of ours, wiped it across the shop floor with enough vigor to know that it could now only haunt my dreams, and tossed it in the trash.

The one good thing about a dead day is that you have fuck-all to do when it's time to get going; nothing in the trash, so no trash to pull, and no cash drop to calculate. I could only hope that the tattoo gods would shine down on me the next day, but if you thought about it too much they wouldn't bring you a damned thing to teach you a lesson. It was with these little superstitions that ran universal through the whole tattoo industry churning through my mind, and my empty stomach flopping against itself, that I locked up the shop.

The rain had eased up and a cold damp hung heavy in the dark. While I was lighting my ciga-

rette, a raspy hiss cut through that made me think another storm was tracking me from down the street. Shitty days always fight to get shittier.

I cracked my neck to keep calm as I approached the little shit focused on his spray-paint can at George's shutter. He'd only made it as far as "GO HOME CHI" before his brain had stalled and he fought to remember how to spell the derogatory. As it was, he stood there, spraying little puffs of orange into the air as the last brain cells not incapacitated by acetone fought the good fight.

"It's n-k," I said and ground my cigarette into the sidewalk.

The dickhead actually turned with a smile at my helpful pointer. One of the eyes was a bit cocked, and the far left incisor on the top was missing; some equally abhorrent dickhead had sloppily tattooed a P under his right eye, as though it was some gang sign. If it was, I had never heard of it, and if I had never heard of it, it didn't mean shit in the city.

"What's up with that one letter, though?" I didn't have to ask it, but it made it more fun that way.

120

BETTER LIVING
THROUGH BLOODSHED

He turned toward his handiwork, and as he criticizing the lettering, in one smooth movement, I grabbed the greasy hair on the back of his head and threw my whole weight into the shutter. Something broke between my hand and George's shutter, with that stabbed-dog, high-pitched guttural that comes with something breaking, but I kept a firm grip on him. Another throw brought a more nasal noise from him, the third was more of a groan, and with the fourth, and my shoulder starting to scream, it was more of that thoughtless bubbling blood. I dropped him onto the sidewalk and shook my arm out; the joys of yesterday are the labors of today.

He lay there coughing blood onto the wet, dark sidewalk, so at most it was assault; you never know how it's going to play, and most of the time breathing is a good sign, this time included. If you murder 'em, then they never get a chance to learn their lesson. There was a second, alright, maybe more than a second, that I considered running his pockets, but even a piece of shit like that would have enough problems when he woke up without having to look for his ID. Anyway, his pants were

probably covered in meth-laced piss by that point, since you had to have a penchant for some type of hard drug to enjoy graffiti and bigotry at the same time.

I skipped over Dead Heat, preferring a faster means of payment, and settled on the real cash. Bitter rain pummeled the side of my face, forcing me to pull my hat low. Every street in the country has a sucker walking it, city or farm, mountain or plains, an easy paycheck with almost no risk if you know how to find it. Gamblers are simple to pick out, that sad desperation seeming to drip off of them in a trail, but, while they're simple enough, you don't want to catch them after they're bust, and if they're flush make sure they aren't carrying anything for protection; fear plus money equals a quick trigger. A college kid could go either way so far as the wallet is concerned, but they're more size than ability in a scrap across the board, and if nothing else you can lift a nice watch that'll get you a couple bucks. Drunks are easy targets, but you need to make sure that you catch 'em after the punchy phase, when the bile's already creeping up and the energy is slipping down. You never

fuck with local civilians, that's just bad karma and an easy way to get a shit name on the street. They didn't sign up for war, and while most of them are smart enough to know the game, their names aren't on the board. You want to be Robin Hood, not a viper in the nest. Next time John Law comes around, you want alibis at every door you darken.

At Caesar's I cut down to Atlantic. On a shitty, spring night, the pickings on Pacific were too thin. They were there, but I didn't want to work for it if I didn't have to. The shoobies would be a block over if they weren't in the casinos or a hotel bed. You didn't fuck around in the casinos without a solid hustle if you could help it. Along the strip of failed and failing clubs, secretly bustling porn joints, and bars that you never drank in but got take out from all the time, I saw a mark.

The little puff of hair defending itself against the rain through some surely-toxic chemical substance, spray-on tan looking splotchy even at a distance, overly-tight MMA t-shirt looking even more overly-tight because of the damp, basketball sneakers that had never seen a basketball court doing a Fred Astaire stumble side to side across the

sidewalk. It was as though the gods of hustling had crafted this prey just for me. From a distance the rain obscured any real distinguishing features, but as we closed the distance the face grew clearer.

Through the wind and rain and splashing slop, I could smell his cologne at twenty feet; at ten the foggy eyes, a little cocked with inebriation, grew clearer. I recognized this mass of dumb muscle swerving slowly toward me. His little lackey was nowhere to be found, but that didn't mean that he wasn't nearby. If he recognized me and remembered where the shop was, which was unlikely but not impossible, I'd be fucked. But fate favors the bold and there was only one way to find out.

I pulled my head back so my face would be clear, angled my jaw so it would be at the best angle under the streetlights, and aimed right for him. Our shoulders connected with a force that wouldn't be unnoticed, even in his state, and I spun off in a way that would leave me facing him. He spun a bit less, those chunks of sinew and flesh a bit less impervious, but he still eyed me over before he turned away, with a "fucking assholes."

I trailed behind him, the reflective strips at

the bottom of his shirt shimmering in the street-light. The whispering trails of his thought, "fuck-ing city"..."dumb hicks"..."never make it in a real city"..."fucking place is dead", all hit me in the breeze. I pulled my jacket off while walking and flipped it inside out, blaring the glossy, burnt orange lining that I had found obnoxious to the world, I cocked my hat to the side in a way that blurry eyes might mistake for a baseball cap.

"Fuckin' girls and drinks cuz," I said as I slowly, slowly passed. "Not a fucking dude to be found. There's local stronzos but they ain't shit." I could feel him turning his attention toward me. The reflection off of car mirrors and shop windows worked to keep a pace where he was close enough behind me to make sure that I was heard. Still, I made sure to repeat the facts enough times that they would sink into that thick skull.

"Nah cuz, I'm almost there now," I waited for a bus to pass. "Gotta get there while there's still talent." I felt slimy just listening to myself. "Fuck yeah, I got the stuff." I wasn't even sure what stuff, but any stuff would probably appeal to a hapless traveler.

He was damned near on my heels now, and didn't show any signs of passing. I might have thought he was more sober than I had assumed, if it weren't for the wobble of the mile-wide shadow leading before us in the rotting-lemon yellow light of the streetlights. No worries, he wouldn't have to trail me for long.

We hit the head of one of the more particularly dark and dingy alleys in the area, and I stopped to light a cigarette, closing my eyes to the flame. Meat-mountain stopped behind me, not even trying to look busy. This worked better with two people, but one would do. I brought the electric paperweight that my phone would be until I had it turned back on to my face and pretended to be looking up pertinent information. He kept waiting, so I had him hooked.

My stroll kept casual, to stop him from getting worried, as we traveled deeper and deeper into the alley. From the vantage of the entrance, and if you didn't know how it worked, you'd never know that there was a tighter alley that shot off from the end. It just looked like the typical creepy alley, that your typical creepy guy would picture a delightfully de-

BETTER LIVING
THROUGH BLOODSHED

baucherous club in. If you were from there, you'd know that there was only the back door to a shitty Chinese place that had closed the year before. I kicked a few bottles out of the way, you could never trust a bottle to stop someone this big.

When we hit the halfway point of the alley, far enough that any looky-lou's from the street would be out of eye-shot, I found a good spot to play the game. I bent as though I was tying my shoe, a pile of construction refuse piled at my side, and took a tumble. Meat-mountain went to help me up as I felt the rough edges. I'm not sure if it was through general goodwill, or a hope to get into the imaginary club with me. I'm guessing the latter. That half a cinder block was heavier than I expected, as it swung up to his bent head. The sound wasn't what you'd guess from a movie; it's kind of a combination of every noise that the human throat has ever made as the impact hits the skull. He hit the pavement with a real dead weight that actually had me a bit concerned. I threw my shoulder into the weight of his twitching form as I rolled him into a puddle of seagull shit, trash water, and salt. His wallet pulled out bulging as I'd hoped. The watch,

chain, and a few oversized rings would be nice on some rainy day when the heat wasn't so hot on them. A couple of twitches was enough to let me know that he was vaguely alive as I walked away; enough little bubbles blew from his mouth in the shit-water puddle for me to feel fine.

I switched my jacket back over while I walked the far, short strip of the L-shaped alley, straightening my hat. I was a new man. At the corner, I headed toward the sea.

If you ever want to work through a wallet, do it in a casino; no one is ever going to question a desperate glance in a wallet there. I cut down the path between slots and tables, counting out cards in the only useful way that you can count cards in a casino. Three credit and one debit, the cash on the other side of the wallet I'd wait on. The first chance I had, I palmed his ID. A pair of old biddies were working the slots next to each other. I pumped my confidence up a bit and walked over to their old, grey heads. "How's the hustle going, ladies?" I asked.

"What hustle?" Old One asked with more than a bit of bitterness.

BETTER LIVING
THROUGH BLOODSHED

"Well, you ladies look like winners."

"I'd look better if this cheat wasn't hogging the hot machine," Old Two sneered.

"It's not my fault that you're bad luck! As a matter of fact, why don't you move down? I don't want to catch any of your bad juju."

"I'm bad luck? Mom always..."

As they craned their arthritic spines toward each other, lost in an argument that had been rumbling along for the last millennium, I brought my hand over the purse of Old One and let the ID fall into its gaping maw. They were still nipping at each other as I turned off the row of slots and made for the boardwalk. A breath closer to freedom, at the casino entrance I checked both ways for Johnny Law and cut left.

I was out of practice for this kind of work, and the added haste of my coming back into the fold was rubbing me the wrong way. This was a good chunk out of my debt in one landfall, and here I was, watching the wallet sink below the surf of the inlet, knowing it was never to be seen again, feeling shittier than I had in quite a while. These

games are fun when you're a kid; you've got your friends to share the excitement with, all of the money is just fuck around money, you're a kid, you'll never get caught, because, in the mind of a kid, adults think all kids look the same. At the moment, I didn't have any of those bullet points working for me. Call it jitters, call it having more to lose, call the death of invincibility what you will. Crime's never as great when you're desperate and lonely, and I wasn't feeling particularly free or wanted. The realization that that old joy had flown the coop only served to infuriate me further, and in turn put more pressure on the game, stealing a bit more of the fun.

Across the inlet, the million-dollar beach houses of Brigantine were dark, desolate shells, their seasonal occupants unwilling to even contemplate darkening those doorsteps until Memorial Day. The lights that weren't blown flickered on the dull, grey arch of the bridge, cars droning over slowly after a casino shift-change. Someone said that sharks had started breeding again in the inlet. I couldn't begrudge them a place to fuck, but the last thing this city needed was a toothy moat to

separate the downtrodden from wealth.

Some of you might be wondering why I didn't go and slap down the whole grand and some change on twenty-five red, like every movie would suggest in times of need, but then I might as well just go and hand back that meathead's money and ask if there's no hard feelings. You think I'm a criminal? Well, there might be some truth to that, but there's no bigger crook in the world than a casino. Well, maybe a lawyer, but at least they try to give you something for your money occasionally. Casinos only give you the illusion of a thing, they dangle the hope of an inconceivable dream on the end of a stick, the dream of escape from the hammering blows of generational poverty, but the stick's always a bit too long for you to reach. Figured out how to break the stick? Counting cards? Just daring to be good enough at a game to have the odds in your favor? Have the inconceivable thought that maybe, perhaps, the casino should give something occasionally for all of the money that they take for no reason? Well, that's the quick path to a cement room in the basement where your hands end up not so great at holding cards or shaking dice or

rubbing one off ever again. What happens when they finally let you out? Well, Johnny Law's there to escort you away from the premises and you've got a blacklist across every gambling house on the island. I might be a hypocrite, it's not like I don't make my easy money in those garish halls of sin on a nearly nightly basis, but it's a sucker that leaves money in the hand of the devil free of charge.

The salt air was thick and stagnant in the shop that early in the morning, a cool dew slipping around on the varnish under my arms. All was quiet overhead, so at least I had the luck that Angelo was probably still passed out after whatever gut-turning activities he had gotten into the night before. The massage table creaked and groaned and so did my back as I eased myself up and off of it, but my head felt a hell of a lot clearer than it had, like waking after the fever broke. I've never been fond of sleeping in a shop, too many ghosts inhabit them, but any port in a storm. Across the street, the pair of building fronts were all trapped in shadow, but the slim sliver of sky that showed between the two was already a clean blue, so I guessed it couldn't be

too long after sunrise. At some point in the night, the idea must have wormed its way into my mind because by the time my eyes were open again, the plan was fully formed.

I hustled to get my shit together and get out of there because, even though we were closed on Sundays, if that greedy prick upstairs saw me down there he would find one excuse or another for us to open up. Us being me. And I had work to attend to, so I couldn't have that.

The sky was clear, but the bone-deep chill that hung after so much rain brought a smile to my face. That would work just fine.

I packed my backpack at the apartment and threw on an old hoodie that someone had left at some point in the years before I had lived there. A hoodie was good because of the universality of them this time of year, someone else's hoodie was better because it would be gone by the end of the day; plus, no one would pick me out in a photo, because with my build I look like an idiot in a hoodie and, hence, never wear them. On the way out, something in the little coat-closet-turned-junk-closet caught my eye. I grabbed the thick roll from

where it sat halfway out of the closet, as if stepping forward for action, shoved it into my backpack, and was out the door.

It didn't take too long to walk to Venice Park, because nothing takes too long to walk to in the city. I kept to the hood on the way, to stay off of any of those stupid home cameras that everyone posts videos from on the internet these days. When did the world become populated with snitches? I didn't know anyone in this part of town, because they had their own shops or basements to get work done, but at this time of day, it was still too early to get into any rough stuff really. So, I just kept the hood up, head down, and worked a zigzag through the blocks.

Venice Park is just a kind of little nothing island that butts against the main island. I don't mean "nothing" in some pejorative "they're nothing" sense because they don't live on the main island. I'm not a New Yorker. I just mean that there's literally nothing to do there; just a few blocks of houses, a church or two, and maybe a park. I'm not sure on that last one. I've only ever gone to the neighborhood to get fucked up at house parties as

a teenager. There was one point of interest about the neighborhood that did stick in my mind, and would serve me well. Right through the center of the little island was a canal and, in the course of many a drunken evening sitting on docks, I noticed that almost every dock had one type of little putter-around boat or another.

I worked my way down to the end of Kuehnle Ave, past the run-down for-rent houses; past the boarded up for sales; past the charred shells where houses once stood; and past those houses that were still a point of pride for the people that lived within, trying to fight back against the approaching veins of deterioration and entropy. A bum was lying against the bulkhead in the parking lot at the end of the street, but he was too far gone to notice if the island was sinking away, so I didn't have much to worry about there. A quick glance over the bulkhead confirmed that it was low tide, those back waterways can get a bit weird, and I got up onto the ledge, went over onto my stomach, and lowered myself down.

The mud stank of death, but I wasn't in any risk of sinking to the center of the earth, never

to be found; the years of trash and old building supplies dumped there saw to that. With my back to the bulkhead, I shuffled over to the first floating dock, damned near grounded with how low the tide was, and from there it was just a few hops to an acceptable vessel. I untied a few lazy knots from the dock cleats, cast off, and let the current pull me down the canal. A quick way to garner all of the attention of the neighborhood would have been to rev that rusty shit engine before eight in the morning. Once I was well into marshes, I grabbed the pull cord and got her going.

When we were out past the water treatment plant, I found a quiet little island of reeds, killed the engine, and pulled her up on the beach. She was only a nine-foot flat-bottom, so it wasn't too much to get her high enough to get done what needed getting done. I grabbed the roll from my bag, tossed the bag back into the boat, and relished the clean tearing sound as the black duct tape pulled away from the roll. I had most of a roll, so there would be plenty to cover all sides above the waterline. The thinking was two-fold. One, I didn't want some poor fuck to get popped

over a job I had done because some Nosy Nelly remembered the ID numbers or color of the boat and John Law tracked it back. Two, just so you don't get the impression that I was going through all of this for purely altruistic reasons, if the owner of this fine vessel should notice it missing for the short time I was borrowing it and called the law, I didn't want to get popped myself before I got everything done.

To my astonishment, the tape seemed to hold to the wet aluminum with no problem, and we were back to skimming across the murky depths in no time flat. I gave Venice as wide a berth as possible when I passed it, keeping the engine to a low hum, and only opened her up when we passed below the tracks; the train rumbled in all slow and tired overhead, chips of paint and cement tinkling down to the schooling fish below.

You know that you're getting into a wealthy neighborhood when the houses look more and more unlivable for their day-to-day needs. Garish structures jutted out halfway into the canal, with canal-water waterfalls cascading over glassed-in

porches in the back, or with ornate spiral stairs rising like deranged waterspouts from the rocks to the second floor. It's a classic case of money over taste, and function is a key element to taste. I mean, the back of one was a solid wall of concrete right up to the seawall, no windows, no door.

The sun had crested the houses on the other side of the canal, and the skin of the water glimmered like the glass from a car wreck. I pulled up to the dock of a place that was sensical enough to have a clearly marked door, but had nice, high privacy fences at either side. Now I just had to hope that my timing was right. By all accounts, if luck was on my side, this should have been just about the time when the owners hadn't yet arrived for the summer, but the help had already been by to stock the house with the finery needed for one of their status. A fountain of a dozen cement koi spitting into each other's mouths was still off for the year, but the windows of a pair of old French doors had been recently cleaned in preparation of the approaching manor lords.

Old doors are nice, but old doors designed for pristine climates and not looked after don't fare

well by the sea. The paint was brilliantly looked after, credit where credit is due, but one little shove showed the telltale signs of rot and ruin beneath. I put the little pry-bar away and, with the handle of one door pushed down, and the other pulled up, a quick bump with my shoulder popped them apart. Easy peasy.

I pulled the doors near to closed, wiped the handles, walked around the side of the house to where to fence came in against the siding, and lit a cigarette. In Ventnor Heights, if an alarm trips, John Law will leave a burning hospital across town to check on your things. The way I saw it, I probably only had a five-minute wait before I could get to work. The cigarette butt stubbed out and securely stashed in my pocket, and after a minute to come to terms with how shoddily they had installed the siding, I went round to the back door again. With the first whiff of that mix of hospital disinfectant and museum-old, I knew that I was in the right place. Electronics are a bad call on a run like this; televisions are too big if they're worth anything; anything small enough to carry probably had a tracker on it these days. Plus, if the heat is on, by the time

you get around to getting rid of it, it isn't worth anything anymore. All hassle, no reward. I didn't see any cameras, but the hood was up and gloves were on just in case. No visible markings.

Bedrooms were the spots to hit. You see, the rich are too vain, lazy, or both to have anything valuable hidden away, and some sense of omnipotence gives the false impression that what they have was granted to them and protected by God himself. That's the problem with never having to work for anything you've ever gotten. I just happened to hit the master bedroom first. Jewelry boxes were first into the bag, box and all. It's not like what I was working on would go unnoticed if I left the boxes. Don't bother looking for cash, they pay for everything with a card on the off chance that there would be a write-off at the end of the year, and it's not like they tip. After a quick glance in the closet, I looked at the far wall for the first time and there, hanging like some forgotten hotel painting, was a god damned Heinrich Kley drawing. If it was a fake, it was a damned good one, but I don't think it was. A real piece of genius art has a certain feel to it, like an electric charge, or a ghost. And

140

here it was, seen for a quarter of the year, if that, and discarded from thought through those colder, darker days. In a great bit of irony, it was one of his drawings of a nobleman looking like a real idiot, but I'm sure that was lost on them. I pushed the annoyance away and moved on. I didn't have a bullet-proof art guy, and this was business.

Ugly ornaments and little statues were scattered around the guest rooms, but they all felt of pure silver, so in they went. Downstairs, the living room was all but worthless; in the big dining room, the walls painted that stereotype sloppy-white you'd see in gaudy magazines of beach-house decor, a giant china cabinet covered a whole wall. Every shelf, every nook, every corner was filled with one or another piece of austere accoutrement for proper entertaining. Because who doesn't need a full serving set, complete with gold-rimmed cups and ornate silver, for when friends drop by your beach house?

As I was closing up my bag, a silver carving knife, set in a mahogany holder with, surely real, ivory inlays, called to me. Shit. No, this is a bad idea. God damn it.

I went back into the bedroom with all of my smart intentions shitting the bed. I'm not one for buying the hype of price, but fuck did that knife feel nice in the hand. It felt even better as I dinged up the blade prying away the little metal tabs that held the frame against the backing board. When the frame came away and I had a good look at it, I couldn't hold back an exasperated sigh. Plastic. A fucking plastic frame for a Kley. These assholes deserved all of this and more.

I was half tempted to draw a turd onto the backing board before I put it back into the frame, but thought better of it. People have been caught for far less stupid things.

In a house full-to-the-brim with the pretty but useless, I finally found something to transport the Kley in the kitchen: a silicone cutting mat, a little bigger than I needed was wedged into the side of a cabinet, and a roll of plastic wrap sat soggy under the sink. I took the wrap and pulled a long strip across the counter, leaving it attached to the roll, sat the silicone mat on the plastic, and the Kley on that. A quick roll of the mat and I had an improvised tube, which seemed still enough; taking the

plastic wrap around five or six more times and it would be waterproof enough to get it home safe.

I ran the boat aground behind some forgotten construction on the main island, not too far from Venice. The tape was a bit of a bear to get off, but better that than too easy en route. I took the hoodie off and wiped down anything that I might have touched which, on a boat, could be pretty much anything. At the bottom of my bag, I found the other bag, the same size to make sure that everything would fit, but a clearly different color, and transferred the goods over. Into the old bag went the wad of tape and hoodie, and the whole parcel took a vacation under a board in the construction dumpster.

The track jacket that I'd worn under my hood was a bit damp with exertion, but with the coming of a light rain I was glad for it—I just hoped that the wrap job I'd done would hold. That's the sort of shit that you can't know until the end though, so there's no sense in worrying about it until said end. It's that kind of thinking that gets you preoccupied, and preoccupied is sloppy, sloppy is popped.

Until then, it would just be Schrodinger's Kley. It was only ten blocks or so to the station, an approaching train whistle blowing as I walked, but you had to hoof every one of the ten, no back way in, no shortcut to be found, and for some reason that lack of options always pissed me off. This was the land of freedom, so any one thing that lacked the appearance of choice struck me as authoritarian, and a slippery slope to the life of any other choice going the way of the dodo. Still, silver linings, doors and windows, I had to take advantage of everything that I had, so I spent the walk thinking over the back and forth of any way that the very-soon-to-come negotiations could go. They were still just rough guidelines. You can't get too locked into a back-and-forth, or boxing yourself into the way anything could play out for that matter, or you'll never have room to win. You play by anyone else's rules and you're already at the disadvantage. The one nice thing about living next to those cash and viscera churning behemoths is knowing to look out for who makes up the way that you have to play in life.

I used one of the ticket machines in the sta-

tion, even though they're a fucking nightmare, because the more that you can fall into a faceless crowd, the less likely you are to be picked out by the powers that be. Even the stupidest thing, a stuttered word, a sneeze, a tattoo, which I was covered in, would be more than enough for a teller to remember you if your luck was shit; which mine was starting to feel like. A quiet corner, not so cramped in to make waves but not far enough away to stick out, was where I plopped down until they announced the train. When that fateful call (which all calls are when you think about it) finally came, I made sure to keep to the center of the pack. Fuck a good seat. A traveler with a good seat is the first seen by a conductor; you want to catch them when they're already getting hypnotized by the stream of bodies.

I took a seat in the busiest cluster of weary and broken strangers grouped up in a car toward the back, popped my ticket into the little slot on the seat in front of me, and tilted my head down and away in feigned slumber. A ticket for a station a stop farther than mine, which was the next that we would be hitting, would stop any concern about

my being asleep but not be a noticeable difference if I got off in advance. The bag sat snugly between my knees. I was just a strung-out gambler that had finally hit a wall. Nothing new, and it never would be leaving that town.

With the announcement of Absecon station approaching, I gave a little stretch, grabbed my bag, and padded toward the doors. There's no magic to leaving a train well, so I won't pretend that there is.

We streamed out onto the concourse, and the change in wind hit me like a wet wall. It wasn't bad, like a Philly summer, but there was a change in the way that the asphalt oil lingered in the air, the way the exhaust from the White Horse Pike seemed to billow up toward us, that seemed to cut like a knife, as though summer was already here in full force.

I walked down the side of the pike, the sea-grasses whispering at my side and the highway thrum drumming along its black stream, until I got to Joe's. His place was on the second floor of a short string of duplexes that hung over the bay; the places of the forgotten or the wanting to be forgot-

ten. Empty chip bags and smaller baggies crowded around the foot of the stairs. I never knew what I would walk into in his place, but at that point I didn't have many choices.

The door was damp with greasy dew as my knuckles rapped against the bubbling, faded paint. The sound of greenheads buzzed through the reeds, trucks coughed and choked along the commute, but from inside came only the silence of the tomb. Fucking Joe. I pounded against the door a little harder, sounding like a cop, but not giving a fuck. Maybe it would get him in gear.

That is, unless he took a dive into the bay off the back porch. I'd probably hear the splash if he did. I was about to start kicking when I heard a clinking clamor from within. I could feel footfalls approaching through the soles of my shoes (Christ this place was a death trap) and just as quickly stop. It's not like he had a peephole, so I'm not sure what he was hoping to accomplish standing there. If anything, if I was someone that he had pissed off, which the area was rife with, that would be the perfect place to catch a bullet. Okay, enough nonsense.

"Yo, idiot! Open the fucking door," I shouted loudly enough to kick his paranoia into opening up.

"Jesus! Neighbors," the face behind a scruff of disheveled hair and beard hissed, as he cracked the door and looked in either direction down the gangway.

"Well, you'd better let me in before they think you have a gentleman caller." I pushed past him into the heavy gloom. Empty soda cups and takeout containers littered his permanently-sticky-looking coffee table; empty enough forty bottles dripped onto the carpet where they had made that clatter; the eternal haze of a house of too poor ventilation and too much weed smoke drifted lazily around. I would say 'much like Joe himself', but he had that all too common, and all too annoying, combination of laziness and paranoid energy that just grates on me. "Well, Joe, this place sure is coming together as a total piece of shit."

"Enough, man. I just need to tidy up a bit."

"There isn't enough gasoline in the world."

"Listen, man, if you're not going to be kind, I don't need that kind of energy."

BETTER LIVING
THROUGH BLOODSHED

He was always going on about energy and vibrations and shit, like he just came out of a Manson family time capsule.

"Again with this shit?"

A big hole in the back of his t-shirt showed a sea of freckles as he walked toward the door mumbling, "You come over way too early for a civilized guest, bringing your bad vibes, man. I kindly ask you to depart."

"Are my bad vibes allowed to stay if they come with a nice payday?"

His whole posture changed as he turned at the mere hint; back straightened, hand pulling his beard into form, eyes lost of their drifting dullness. All business now. "Well, why didn't you say so, friend?"

Everything sat spread out on the coffee table, which had been cleared and wiped in record time, the various metals and gems glinting in the light from a just-pulled curtain. The rest of the apartment still looked like shit, and I'd hate to check under the couch I was sitting on, but that was no business of mine. All that mattered was inventorying, and I knew no one better than Joe at that

job. While going piece by piece, I kept a keen eye on his hands. He wasn't dumb, but you can never trust those types with temptation.

"What's in the wrap?" he asked, glancing at my bag on the couch.

"That's not part of the deal."

"Painting? Drawing?" I would have questioned it, wondering if somehow he had been following me all day, but for a thief like him guessing that was nothing. I'd seen the kid guess how many watches were in a bag before it was even opened. "I wouldn't mind taking a look..."

I smacked the top of his twitchy little hand as it reached over. "Nothing good comes from being nosy, sweetheart."

He looked a little hurt, a bit tempted by the mystery, cogs behind his eyes working at a way to have a peek, but again, he's not dumb and he knew what would happen if I lost my patience.

"You interested?" I asked, while his interest was very-fucking-much there.

"Fuck yeah—" he started. "Of course, I may be."

His new love of speaking properly was a bit

annoying, but as far as tics go in that section of the underworld, his wasn't bad.

"I need my cut in advance," I said.

"That's not how this works."

Real world value? Probably eighty grand, easy. Black market? Fifteen to twenty, no problem if you wait for the right buyer. That kind of math off the top of my head made the next thing I said all the harder.

"Three grand."

"Wait, what?" Joe slid back, knocking an old carton of fries over.

"That's all I want. The rest is yours."

He looked over the spread, unsure how to play the next move.

"That's not your cut..." Those gears sure were working. "You'd get at least—"

"I know how to count. I just need to make a move."

"What's the trick?" His brow furrowed, looking for what I was up to. A hustler is a hustler, and if you're not hustling in a 'too good' situation, then you're being hustled.

"Look," I said, pulling my bag forward. "Even

if all of this shit came out of a cereal box, you could get three times that, all day. If you're not interested—" I brought the bag to the edge of the table and hand over to sweep it in.

"No, no, no," he said, reaching toward my hand. "Don't be so hasty, good chap."

It was early afternoon when I got back into the city and I was already exhausted. I don't know how those nine-to-fivers do it, that early-day sun really does kick the shit out of you. With a rock-hard soft pretzel in hand from the little newsstand, I made my way out of the station and to the curb. I barely had enough for a felony offense on my person, so I felt fine with taking the civilian route, and my legs felt like they were going to dissolve if I braved the trek anyway.

There's little rhyme or reason in the placement of shuttles at the station; god forbid it be one through five with each taking certain blocks in a row. Instead, and I'm only guessing here, someone must have had the novel idea to pay more for the first spot, and the rest of the casino owners mud-wrestled to see what order the rest of the

shuttles came in. It sure as fuck wasn't logic that made these decisions.

I looked over the names of the casinos, on their typographic nightmare signs, and tried to figure out which would be closest to where I had to go, while being earliest in order; no little feat with how my head was feeling. The concussion seemed to be wavering, but my mental stamina was feeling as though it would never bounce back to the 'near mint condition' that I had before. I guess the lucky days were over.

The back was the only row with an open seat, so I cramped myself in between a compulsive gambler in a stained button-down and a tired-looking room service lady huffing in a too-tight uniform. In a lucky turn of fate, the air conditioning was pumping, because I was starting to sweat in the summer-to-come heat that swept off of the mainland. Fuzzy muzak from an out-of-tune station drifted sad over the cracked speakers, and I watched the candy facade of Atlantic City given to tourists pass slowly through dirty windows.

The Pinnacle Hotel lobby had that same 'fam-

ily safe' feel that every lobby has ever had; the soft cornered chairs, the historical photos of historically insignificant moments, the plants that must have been grown at Hotel Lobby Farms, all of it designed to ease long-ingrained tensions, short of Pauly sitting cold and motionless in an over-sized chair in the corner. I might have thought he was dead, not reading, not looking around, if it wasn't for the labored breathing that stretched the arms of the chair compressing him at either side. How long was he just sitting there, thoughtless and determined? How much would it cost someone to pay me to do that? Sadly, not as much as I would like to claim.

"I've got the cash," I said, waiting a surprisingly long time before Pauly acknowledged me.

"I was hoping it would be another couple of days."

What the fuck was he on about?

"Okay, so, can we go up to Giordano's?"

Pauly sighed, looked side to side, and with a great labor pulled himself out of the chair. He waved me ahead, sticking close enough that we looked like old chums, but far enough to put a

154

bullet in me if I tried anything slick, like I wanted back into trouble with this crowd. In the elevator he stuck next to the buttons—I'm not sure why he thought that was imperative—and the seams on his suit jacket bulged under the strain of keeping his arms in.

"I've got a good tailor if you're looking for one," I said.

"I've got a good hole in the marshes if you're looking for one," he replied, with surprising wit.

"Just trying to be helpful."

When the bell dinged and the door slid open, he turned toward me with a cold autonomy that I didn't think he had in him. "Get fuckin' movin'."

Giordano's office looked a lot more comfortable when your skull wasn't damned near split. The sea shimmered under a cloudless sky, those brave pre-season souls were frolicking in water that was probably still ice-bath cold, and Giordano was staring out at a flock of squabbling seagulls at the window, looking like he'd put a bullet in them if he could. No one said anything, so I approached the desk until Pauly started to look a little twitchy.

"Hell of a day," I said with a crack in my voice

that I wished wasn't there.

"A wasted existence, thrashing around like that." I couldn't tell if he was talking about the gulls or the swimmers.'

"I've got what you're owed."

"Always to the point, Mister O'Niell." He almost looked disappointed to have to turn toward me. Standing and with a clear head, he didn't look near as unstoppable as he had when I was wobbling in that chair, but no one ever does.

"You're a busy man, and I'd hate to waste time," I said.

"A lie, but a good one."

"I wouldn't say—"

"Do you know what you learn at a poker table, Mister O'Niell?"

I didn't know if he was asking or waxing rhetorical, so I went with the second. Wrong choice. After a few seconds, a little flame started to pop up behind his eyes. "I'm not much of a gambler."

"In this town? In this temple built around the glory of gaming. How can you not?"

The same thing, which no one ever understood, every time.

"I'm not speaking of some amorphous philosophy," he continued. "What you learn, and nothing else, is how to lie and how to catch a liar."

My natural instinct, at the prospect of being lectured at, brought my hand to my cigarettes but I caught myself early.

"Go ahead, Mister O'Niell and have one."

"Come on, boss," Pauly said from the side of the room.

"Pauly doesn't believe in the merits of smoking anything besides a cigar. Claims the fragrance is undignified, in similar terms, as though the taste of one was superior to that of others. Such a small worldview."

I pulled out a smoke and lit it. If I'm going to call a bluff, it might as be one that makes me a bit less edgy.

"Lying is a fundamental point of human existence," Giordano said. "Sure, it helps to save hurt feelings, to create social bonds, but that isn't what matters. Lying is the basis of survival. From time immemorial, lies have propelled power, and they have brought it crashing down."

I didn't see an ashtray, nor one coming, so I

tapped my cigarette into my cupped hand.

"The Greeks, the Ottomans, the mighty Romans," he went on, "yes, they went to war, they conquered by violence. What would become the Germans, the English, the Irish, all brought to their knees by the Holy Roman Empire, by blade or by choice of their women? But the fights that mattered, those against foes that were their equals, of their own kind... those were battles of deception. Battles of deception, they are battles of dominance, man over man. The play of dominance can go much farther than the show of force, Mister O'Niell."

Typical Italian worship of the Romans. I would never understand it. I mean, where the fuck were the Romans now, besides running a pedophile church?

"That's quite the ideological groundwork that you've built." I ashed into my palm.

"Okay..." Giordano looked over to Pauly with a frown, "you have my money already?"

"Yep," I said and dropped the roll of cash in my pocket, as well as the envelope from Joe on the desk. "Every dime." My cigarette was nearing the

filter.

"Not that I don't trust you, Mister O'Niell," Giordano said, pulling the cash from the envelope. "But I don't trust anyone in this little town."

I took the last drag on my cigarette and saw the interest that Pauly seemed to have from the wall. Giordano, I couldn't tell if he was watching, but the slowness of his counting made me presume that he most likely was. I spit into my palm, in the center of the pile of ash, and pressed the cherry into it. What is the trick that stopped it from hurting? Nothing. It hurts like shit. The trick is not showing that it does when you do it.

"Well, the money that you stole is here." Giordano rubbed his closed lips over his teeth. Was that a tell or an act for me? You don't have to play a game to understand the fundamentals, the same way you don't have to be a plumber to know where a piece of shit goes.

"Alright, well, it was good doing business with you," I said, turning away from the desk.

I made it halfway across the room. "The interest, Mister O'Niell."

"The what?"

"Interest, Mister O'Niell. It's a percentage of profit for loans."

"I know what interest is but—"

"A detail of all of the loans that I provide is an interest rate, for all loans not paid in full by the date agreed upon. Since no payment date was agreed upon, as you know well, then I would think the day my money went missing is a good day to start with."

"I didn't take out a loan."

"For theft, the perpetrator is killed, with their identifiable parts being sent to their close friends or family, the eyes, hands, cock, a week before said friends and family themselves are summarily dispatched. Would you prefer that I consider this a theft?"

If my fist gripped any tighter, the filter and ash would have made a diamond. "No, a loan would be perfectly fine."

"Well then, the interest rate for all loans is thirty percent per day. So, according to my calculations that would be..." he did some pretend calculations, as though he didn't have it on the top of his head. "Yes, it would be seven thousand two

hundred dollars. I won't compound the interest during the initial period, because it seems like an unfair practice to me. But it seems as though you could use a learning experience, so every day from now until I am paid in full will be sure to."

To say that my guts and nuts squeezed to meet somewhere at the base of my pelvis would be an understatement. I'd hustled enough to put me well into the radar of plenty of groups I'd rather go unknown to already, let alone the stir that the work having to pay this would make. I'm not a quitter, this island doesn't let you become one. It's a place where you grow up tough, or you don't make it that far. Even I, with all that the place had taught me, couldn't think of a way to pay this off before the interest crashed over me.

"I don't think I'm gonna be able to cover that," I laid it out flat. I was fucked, and it's always prudent to know when you're fucked.

"That is very unfortunate, Mister O'Niell." His use of my formal name was annoying me more and more, the more I knew I was bent over a barrel. "The capitalist system can be very unforgiving for people who are unwilling to prepare themselves

realistically."

It was time to lie back and think of England, but I hate a fuckin' monarchy. Pauly was smiling as he picked at his nails with a switchblade. The pens of Giordano's desk wavered as my blood pressure tried for a stroke. I'd say I was envisioning a body bag, but I knew that I would never be found in order to end up in one.

"I might be persuaded to absolve the interest," Giordano went on, and my stomach clenched, "if you could retrieve something for me."

How do three people fit on one chair? If you're getting double fucked.

'I'll think about it.' 'Don't think too long.' The words bounced around in my mind as I walked down the boardwalk. Most of the shops had already opened, and the boards were streaming with high school kids relishing in one of their last few free days where the boards were still theirs, before the masses of stopping, confused tourists bunched up traffic and you couldn't go ten feet without some idiot from New York bumping an ice cream cone onto your shirt.

BETTER LIVING
THROUGH BLOODSHED

I was close enough, and didn't feel like carrying a bag around all day, so I decided to stop off at the shop. If Angelo thought that I would be up for working a few hours, well, he was shit out of luck. I pulled out yet another piece of paper that had been wedged into the door, as I opened up. Let's see what the local lunacy has going through the pipeline. 'DO NOT TRUST THEM. LEAVE NOTE IN DOOR IF YOU NEED ME. HA' Well, at least they ended it with a laugh. I didn't like being the looney note depository, but once they latch onto you they don't give up, and there really isn't shit that you can do about it until they get distracted by something else.

The paper with the Kley drawing fit into a little spot in the top of the floor cabinet at my station with the help of some tape. At least I knew that, no matter how much time and coke he had, Cousin Tommy would never find it. The creak of a bed fighting an immense weight told me that Angelo was probably just getting up, so I took that as my cue and bolted for the door.

A black car was parked across the street, probably looking for some cheap alone time with one

of the crackheads, but if that was their hope, they shouldn't try with such an undercover-cop-looking car. From the look of the goon in the front seat, chomping on a carrot stick, it was no cop. As I was glancing over at the car, just clearly enough to get him moving along, Q turned onto the block.

"What's goin' on kid?" I asked.

He turned to look over his shoulder, like someone had crosshairs on him, and stopped a few feet away. "Yo man, I can't be talkin' to you like that."

"The fuck? Since when?"

"Since you pissed off whoever you pissed off, since then."

"Shit, that's all taken care of. Nothing to worry about there."

"Not taken care of enough. Look man, I don't like this shit, but you're a marked man. 'Til I hear otherwise, motherfuckers can't even be seen around you if they want to stay above the dirt."

"It ain't that serious," I said, really feeling like I was in the bottom of a hole.

"Serious or not..." Q shrugged. "You get your house in order and we're good. I just... I gotta look out for mine."

BETTER LIVING
THROUGH BLOODSHED

"I feel ya. No worries."

He didn't look happy about the turn of events, but things happen the way that they happen, and there isn't much that you can do about that. All I knew, at that moment, was that if they got to Q and could turn him, then I had to play ball.

After paying off the minimum that would get this horrid phone turned back on, as communication was seeming a bit more vital at the moment, I barely had more than a hundred bucks and a matchbook in my pocket. I needed two things: a good angle to talk to Jen about the job—and with how I seemed to be in her graces at the moment, it had better be a damned good angle—and a way to make the vague outlines of a plan Giordano had given me work. There was a bit of a tight budget in my pocket to think up a plan at most bars, my usual go-to for planning, but more than enough for the best bar in the world.

Some change clanged against the bottle in my pocket as I stepped down the wooden stairs and onto the sand, my sock-stuffed shoes dangling in my hand. I was no shoobie, after all, no matter the

circumstances. The sea still held the murky grey of winter, and after a moment or two of standing, the deep cold permeated the warm upper layers of sand under my feet. I took a seat on a dry stone from a long-washed-away jetty, cracked the bottle of whiskey, and toasted that the plotting-gods might bless me with a way to get out clear.

It was only about a third of the way through the bottle, the sea picking up in force with the rising tide, that my phone started buzzing. The intricacies of the plan were far from smooth, but a foundation was putting itself together for me. As for Jen, well, the only way I had any chance of getting her to go along with it was to play it straight, she was too damned smart to fall for any nonsense, but if I was her would I want to help me with how I'd been acting? Not too sure. The phone didn't seem like it would quit with the seizures any time soon, so I pulled it out of my pocket, my brow creasing Grand Canyon deep when Mary's name popped up.

"How's my favorite aunt?" Mary never called. The whole reason I had her number was to check in if I was working out of town.

BETTER LIVING
THROUGH BLOODSHED

"—broken glass everywhere and I'm afraid I'm bleeding. Oh, dear. Would you be a doll and come by if it's not too much trouble?"

I was half out of breath by the time I reached Mary's, bouncing up the front steps on tingling knees, and forced myself to take a breath or two before knocking on the door. The way I was feeling I would have pounded on it like a cop and scared her half to death. I lit up a cigarette, took a couple of deep drags, flicked the waste of tobacco into the gutter, and tapped on the door.

Some people can keep up a good face no matter the situation, and Mary was one of the best. Dead dog? Fine. Car got stolen? No problem. The thing is, when your whole career is keeping up a good face, you can spot the cracks from a mile away. She kept herself half-hidden behind the door, even as I was making my way in, as though it could block her forever, and that defensiveness just raised the hair on the back of my neck more.

"So, where'd your window go for early retirement?" I asked, wondering if she could tell how phony my smile and charm were.

"Oh, just through here," she said. "You know, I feel so silly calling you over for this. I just, I got startled is all." Her hand was gripping an old kitchen towel, but none of the red stuff was showing, so I figured it wasn't emergency room bad.

"You gonna let me take a look at that?"

"Never mind that. Just help me clean up a bit, doctor."

The living room looked like an early frost had taken it, all shimmering glamour of a million glass shards coating everything flat enough to hold it. The ocean breeze came in, slipping over the jagged blades of glass and shuffling the pages of the magazines on her coffee table. Whoever the dumb shit kid was that had done this, he was in for a bad day. Age is a very secondary concern when it comes to these games. I cracked my knuckles as quietly as I could and tapped a big piece of glass toward the center of the room with my shoe. In the middle of the floor was a heavy, glass ashtray.

"I just don't have an idea who would do such a thing," Mary said.

I crouched down, lifting the ashtray and turning it round in my hand. Good quality. At the base

of it was nice, clear printing. 'I'm at the Pinnacle Hotel, Wish You Were Here!'

Mary might not have an idea, but I sure as fuck might.

Pauly was sitting in the same chair that I had last seen him in when I got to the lobby. His suit was a different color, but the cut was just as shitty. In his hand, he was turning a little metal tube round and round, like some fucking magpie with a shiny piece of plastic.

"You gonna take me up?" I said, keeping far enough back that the urge to shatter his pudding face didn't overwhelm me.

"Mr. Giordano is a bit preoccupied at the moment." He wouldn't even bother to look up at me, just kept spinning that little tube and tapping his foot. "So, I'll be working as his intermediary."

"Good for you, learning new words. Tell him I'll do it."

"You're lucky Mr. Giordano is such an understanding man."

"Seems like a lot of that is going around," I said and started walking off.

"It was me? You wouldn't have got off so easy," he said a little loud for its lack of subtlety.

I gripped the ashtray in my jacket pocket tight as the light hit me. That midnight electricity that makes you want to grit your teeth until they crack or close the throat of the next breathing soul that passes was coursing up and down my spine. I knew it was a dumb reaction, I was of sound mind and body, but I just didn't want to stop. I wanted to play every move wrong on purpose until the lengths of my madness were unfathomable. I wanted to light a cop car aflame and sign my name in the gasoline. I wanted to drag every casino owner out of their offices and tie them all to a big fucking anchor off the coast. I wanted to blow up the bridges and just wait for things to get bad bad on the island. That type of unpredictability is invigorating, like if you hit a certain level of mad, then they'll never be able to stop you, because they just wouldn't be able to get their heads around the whole damned point of it all.

I made my way down Pacific eyeballing every hard-man hoodrat that I could spy, gave a shitty smirk to every try-hard out-of-towner pissed off in

front of casinos. To my rare good luck, which felt very much unlucky at the time, not a one could be found to act on my assaults of uncouth. That's the way that it goes, though. Finding hard times is like pulling teeth when that tickle in your knuckles will be eased by only one thing.

The lack of a doorman at the Ocean View was further proof of that piece of shit guardian angel on my side. What was the opposite of a guardian angel? An absentee demon? I needed one of those with the quickness.

Some old piece of shit was working Dead Heat that I hadn't seen enough times to know the name of. I walked to my accustomed spot, put a twenty on the bar, and waited. He just went on leaning there, at the other end of the bar, licking his finger and flipping the page of a beat-up, old, pharmacy paperback. It was a bit early for a rush, but there wasn't a damned soul in the place, and I was starting to understand why.

"Hey pop, can I get a drink?" I asked.

He just put up his finger, eyes still scanning left to right, like that was the appropriate course of action. Time ticked, the muted TV played a base-

ball game that was too fuzzy to pick out the teams, and the jukebox waited for some poor soul who was so sad that he would endure such surroundings just for the company. Sure, I was a bit testy, but I think I was justified in the acid bubbling up from my guts as I waited.

"Hey!" I said, with a tone I hadn't considered right for a bar since I got legal to drink.

He looked up at me with the shock of a coma patient coming to.

"I'm not here for the ambiance," I said, a bit more controlled. "Can I get a drink?"

He gave a big huff, like some fucking ancient baby, and put his book down, hobbling over about as slow as you could get without going backwards, and asked me what I was having.

"Double scotch rocks, and none of that pour-and-a-half shit, pal."

"Tough guy, huh?"

"Doesn't seem possible today, pop. Just start pourin' before I have to test it."

He did the big act of showing how high each of the two pours was, like I gave a fuck how theatrical he wanted to be, and slid my drink over, more

172

rocks in it than Mount Saint Helens. I was tempted to only tip him a buck, because that's about how useful he was, but if I was finally gonna get a chance to hit someone, I wanted to save it for a challenge to hit. I slipped a five from my change about as far from him as I could easily manage, and made my way through piss alley. He might have said something as I passed through, but I had some serious mufflers on at the time.

It was the downtime shift when I came in, which meant the dancers just sitting in booths around the place. The condemned one on schedule to be dancing, sitting on the stage with legs dangling over the edge, eyes locked on her phone. Even the DJ was playing music slow and quiet, like some half-clothed wake was taking place.

Jen was seated with a couple of other girls in a booth, I didn't know too many of the girls on this early shift, and she barely took notice as I took a seat next to her.

"Hey, can we talk?" I asked at a lull in conversation.

"I don't think so."

She was more pissed at me than I thought.

"Come on, Jen."

"Oh, it's Jen now?"

"It's serious now."

"It wasn't serious before? You take me out, talk all of this shit, and right when I think something is happening, radio silence. You're a real piece of shit, Phil."

"Some shit went down that I didn't want you getting involved with."

Her scoff was loud enough to be heard in New York at that.

"I'm not bullshitting. It's serious shit, real serious. I wouldn't have even let you into the periphery—"

"Oh, you wouldn't let me in, why thank you, Mister O'Niell!"

It took a beat for me to keep down my composure.

"You know damned well that that's not what I meant, Jen."

"How am I supposed to know a damned thing about you, Phil?"

Her voice was getting high and she was making me sound like a real asshole, but it wasn't as

though I didn't deserve any, or all, of it.

"That's something we can talk about, but something happened to Mary."

"You dickhead."

I went through the whole damned thing. It felt weird going line for line like that. It didn't feel natural to give so much away without getting anything in return. I hadn't described every inch of a situation with that detail since I was explaining a field trip in fifth grade.

At sitcom timing, Lucky Tom came over just as I was finishing up, Jen still having that venom flicker in her eyes but with the island-resignation-bitterness that we all had for our lot in this world.

"You know cocktails aren't allowed in this establishment," he said, arms folded over his pigeon chest.

"I'm not fucking L&I, Tom," I said.

"I'm sorry, sir, but I'll have to ask you to leave the premises." The grin on his face was a mile wide. It was then that I knew that he knew my status. "We go by the books here."

"If that's the way that you want to play it,

Tom."

He was having too much fun with this new-found power. "I'm not playing anything, sir. You're in clear violation of multiple—"

"Alright, Alright. Fuck sakes, Tom." I turned to Jen, who luckily looked as exasperated as I did. "Meet me outside?"

"Jenny here is on—"

"Fuck off, Tom," she gave him that 'you're dead' look that I was glad to have off my mug. "I'll be out in a second," she said to me.

I was done up in my most normal, but not sloppy, attire; high-priced but off-the-rack button-collar shirt, dress pants but with some pleats thrown in, oxford shoes in that too-warm brown that only dentists and the blind must buy. Just the perfect ensemble of a vapor to the security cameras. My gin and tonic was mostly water, but that was a good sign, I just looked like your everyday rube to the floor, and posted up by a pillar beside a trashcan; the only combination of the two that I could readily find.

Jen was doing her work, and doing it like a

pro. She really was a dream to watch work. The mark was damned near rubbing himself down on the gambling floor, his bald head sweaty above the ring of light brown, his paunch billowing heavy over the gaudy leather belt. She ran a finger down the buttons of his shirt and a spark ran through my spine. Get it the fuck together, kid. I took another sip of my drink and the melted ice had just made it holly-leaf water. Alright, enough time in one place. I plopped down in front of a machine that gave me a good view and threw in a dollar into the nickel slots; high enough to not be noticeable at my age, I wasn't at the penny machines with Goerge Washington's school chums, but low enough to keep the cocktail servers away. From the look on baldie's face, I could tell there was some disagreement, whether on price or decorum, and I had to fight every urge to storm over and settle it. Jen was a pro, Jen was a pro. I took a deep breath and leaned down a bit and took a little hit off of my flask. A pull on the arm and nothing.

It looked like they had made nice, because baldie had a big old smile and was brushing the buttons at Jen's navel. Get to work. I lit a smoke

to give my hands something to do and pulled the slot arm again. Jen rubbed the bulldog cheek and pink flamed up across his face. This would be easy. He pulled out his wallet and my balls got tight. Can't have this fuck up too soon. Jen gave a fake laugh and pressed his hand down, nothing outside of the room. Out of a grubby pocket, he pulled a spotted handkerchief and blotted his head. First-time jitters, or just a dumb fuck that never got honest enough with himself to get comfortable. If you're going to have vices, then own 'em. Nods exchanged, fingers brushed cloth, and I pulled the arm.

Jen put her hand on his lower back. Baldie pulled the smile of someone that hasn't gotten his dick wet in twenty years. The faces rolled on my screen. They turned to leave. I got my bag ready and angled myself, and the machine put out a racket. Everyone stared at me, the machine kept clanging, and Jen wandered off. As her gorgeous back shimmied away her fingers flashed; five, three, fist, two, five. Eighth floor, room eight-twenty-five, in the other hand she held a bag that was small enough that I always wondered how she held so

BETTER LIVING
THROUGH BLOODSHED

much shit in it.

The pit boss came over to share in the revelry. It's amazing what they want you to think a hundred bucks will do. Jen wandered off with baldie toward the elevator, the crowd pulled in tighter, and I tugged the ticket from my machine, while the oldies pushed in further. I gave my best 'oh geez' bashful smile, splashed my drink a little, and squeezed my way out as the degenerated battles for my seat and the pit boss fought to keep composure in the crowd.

I wanted to give them ten minutes to get everything started and avoid the cameras finding a connection, I'd usually tail closer in case anything went south, but I couldn't see much threat in that tub of butter, so I strolled off to a less frantic side of the floor.

I must have been looking less comfortable than I thought because, as I leaned against a pillar, a cocktail waitress snaked her way over to me. It's never a good sign to be getting noticed so soon into a hustle, and I would have usually pulled out, but we were too far in already and it had to be seen to the end. I didn't say no to the drink, I would

have enough reason to be conspicuous by the end of the play, and lit a smoke.

She came by with a smaller-than-average rocks glass filled lower-than-average and I tipped what I figured the average 'middle of nowhere is home' would tip, feeling strange welcoming the look of disappointment. I took down half of the barely tan scotch with a lack of surprise, slots never get much more than water, and started a slow inspection of the slots. Rubes always have that look, like staring down a machine will give away some secret code that that specific piece of machinery is the one begging to hit big every time. I worked over toward a main path through the floor, wrapped my glass in the ticket, finished the smoke water, and tossed them both into the trash. There was a good chance that the bag would get pulled before anyone knew that something had gone down, and it was better to be out that hundred than to go away for it.

The elevators were in a bank along a particularly depressing section of hallway, lights dull, ashtrays kicked with dents, and unsavory stains on the gaudy carpets in front of the doors. I hit the little arrow up but, when an Asian family came

BETTER LIVING
THROUGH BLOODSHED

up, I decided I had to tie my already-tied shoes; waving along their aggressive willingness to wait. After a wait that had a trickle of sweat creep down the back of my collar, another, now empty, elevator pulled into place. I went in casual, but brushed the front of my pants to keep my face out of view, and hit the worn-down eight. I pulled out my phone, funny that the stupid thing was useful for once, and kept my posture bad for the rest of the ride. I heard her voice before I got halfway down the hall.

I forced myself not to run. Running pulls attention on the cameras. Attention is never good. As I got near, I saw an arcade ticket sticking between the door and frame where the lock would be. That was the smart move, not that I was surprised. A keep-it-casual look back down the hall, and I slid into the room, pulling the ticket in with me and sliding it into my pocket. Jen was frantic, which got me cool. Some folks feed into the feel of the room, and some box themselves away to fix it.

She was pacing the room, decked out in her best; silk stockings, leather corset, cat-o-nine still hanging from her hand. The mascara had stayed in place, her cheeks red not from exuberance, her

line of sight was somewhere three rooms over.

"Jen," I said, taking it slow to move in front of her. "Jen."

Her breath was heaving, and I was sure that the corset wasn't helping. I waved a hand in front of her, but she might as well have been a swaying statue. She didn't look to be in any immediate risk of falling so I went for one of the plastic-wrapped glasses and filled it in the bathroom, wondering where the fat prick had got to, and what he had done to get her this worked up. On the way out of the bathroom, I found out.

I was halfway across the room, trying to keep a steady hand so as to not lose any of Jen's water, when a little glimmer caught the corner of my eye. Peeking out from the far side of the bed, the face of a watch shone as my shadow passed, a plump hand attached to it laid still on the rough, tan carpet. I wasn't in the know enough to take anything for granted, so I played it cool and made it over to her.

"Jen," I said, mouth close to her ear, her perfume filling my nostrils. "What do I need to know about him?"

BETTER LIVING
THROUGH BLOODSHED

It was like I wasn't there, but my words were a ghost, because at the mention of the mark, a tic of anxiety worked its way into her eye. I placed her hand around the glass, took a heartbeat to make sure that it would stay in the upright position, and worked my way slow around the bed, the blade coming quiet out of my pocket. Halfway around, I put the blade away. The state that this piece of shit was in made him much more of a threat than a blade could handle.

He was face down, but it wouldn't be the first time someone had played possum around me when they'd fucked up with a girl at a private party, so I eased my heel down on the little bones of his hand, pressing and twisting until just before I would have felt the quick little pops of bone through my foot. I pulled on his shoulder and turned him over, his hand working loose from his collar as he flopped, the restraint of the ball-gag tucked under one of the points of his collar. The handcuff clanked as his arm hit the carpet with a high-pitched tinkle. Alright, things had gone about as south as things go in these situations. Not exactly the flat-tire-south most folks would relate to, I know, but not

an unheard-of outcome in our world.

Eyes closed, two deep breaths. Panic and an unnecessary sense of rush, that's what fucks you up. I blame the movies for it; this idea that John Law has some magic ball that lets them know exactly when crimes have been committed, makes people sloppy. Jen hadn't been loud enough to raise any flags, especially not for casino standards. So, after a little cleanup, short of us fucking up on the egress, there was just a fatty on the floor with no signs of violence. Happened every day on the island. Believe it or not, casino goers aren't notorious for their health standards.

I went through every pocket, inner and outer, pulling each clean. Unbuttoned and buttoned his shirt and pants for any hidden points of interest, rubbing every button clean after getting him back into his best. There's really no point in worrying about DNA most of the time, it's not like most cops have the resources to test for it even if they wanted to. If it looks natural at all? Those chances drop to zero. Super-cops aren't really a thing in real life. Most cops are just some average-intellect asshole who didn't know where else to go for a job,

and do you know what happens when you work too hard and stir up the status quo? That's when you end up on the wrong side of friends. Cops only care about cop friends. Didn't you ever wonder why the thin blue line exists?

His wallet was mostly random cards, of the business and credit sort, which I wiped all of after handling; any business cards that looked like they might pertain to our line of work went into my pocket. Things had changed very much very quickly. This wouldn't be a robbery, no matter how much fun we could have with those little plastic rectangles. Now, it just mattered what happened.

Jen was still where I had left her, but the water was a little lower and she seemed to only be looking one or two rooms away. It was a start. I came over and knelt in front of her.

"Hey Jen," I said, and her eyes caught mine. "Where's the cuff key?"

Her hyperventilating was easing up, but her hands still twitched in her lap.

"Listen," I said with more force than I'd use with her, but these weren't casual circumstances. "You can lose it when we're outside, darlin'. Right

now I need to do my job, and I can't do my job without you." I squeezed her hand real slow and gentle. "Now, where's the cuff key?"

She pointed to the place where the end table touched the bed on the floor and I went onto my hands and knees. I dug my hand blind under the bed skirt, brushing away the dust and bedbugs, until I found the little piece of cold metal. The stiff was just getting stiffer and I made a few adjustments to his body to make it seem more natural after I clicked the cuff from him and undid the buckle of his gag. They both went into my pocket with the key, I looked him over once more and went back to Jen, making sure to take my time; rushing seems nervous, and the last thing you want to be around someone losing it is nervous.

"Hey, darlin'." I put my hand onto her fingers fidgeting with the hem of her leather digs. "What happened?"

That's when she unloaded. It had seemed normal enough, just your usual bondage guy trying out what he would never try with his wife, but as soon as the cuffs were on and the whip came out, shit had gone south. The writhing and thrashing

had come along, which Jen had tried her best to accommodate for. Some of those tie-up guys can get pretty into the act, hoping the more they struggle, the more the girl will punish 'em. Bad luck for him that it wasn't an act. She only realized what the deal was when she got a look into his eyes.

Through the violence of hands smashing about, Jen had managed to work one hand free and then backed off fast as he shot up. His hand at his throat, Jen kept saying. The mark threw himself onto the floor and dug into his bag, digging through until he pulled an inhaler out and put it to his mouth. Jen had already been backing up by then, her chest getting caught up in all of the confusion. The thing didn't seem to do the job though, because he kept wheezing and shaking his hand before he gave up the ghost.

I walked back over to the body and took another look around. Nothing but the usual casino furniture, besides the body that is. His wrists looked fine from the weird bondage padding, and the sides of his mouth weren't red at all; we got lucky that he was still fully dressed or it would be a nightmare moving that much fat around. Feeling a

bit easier I lowered myself over his body, not wanting to move him around too much, smelling the shit that he had left in the pants that hadn't had the chance to come off. An acrid stench was coming off of him from those last seconds of terrified fight. Lifting the bed skirt, the lamp at the far side lying on the floor gave off enough light to see a little object lying there in the darkness. I stretched out a hand and wasn't near, a little closer to the body and I almost touched it, face against his and I could brush the object with my fingertips. I dug my body further, his cooling lips against my ear, and forced myself down. The little object came clean into my hand and into the light. With the mouthpiece next to my palm, I worked the action of pressing the tube into the casing and didn't feel anything. Well, that's not how an inhaler should work.

"Jen, darlin', get into your street gear please," I said as I went back into the bathroom, glad to see clarity in her eyes.

I unraveled a long line of toilet paper from the roll, tore one piece free, and sat the piece on the counter. Out in the room, Jen was pulling on her

pants and I averted my eyes; it seemed indecent to see her like that in this situation. I shoved her work clothes and dress clothes into the bag with the gag and cuffs, wiping down the big dresser top with the toilet paper, and worked my way around the room rubbing clean all of the commonly touched places that could hold a print. The knobs on the lamps were ridged, so we were good there, the counters were print magnets but an easy clean. I took Jen's glass and poured the water onto the carpet before wiping it clean, pressing the stiff's palm onto the glass half a dozen times and his lips to the rim, before depositing it next to the puddle.

I lifted the single piece of toilet paper, pressed down on the handle of the toilet, and dropped all of the paper in. Out of the bathroom, I saw Jen up and going, but not in the way I expected.

"Jen, darlin', we gotta get going," I said as she shifted the bedside table around. I was pretty sure that she'd cracked on me. She squatted down and seemed to be hugging the table. "Jen, we gotta—"

"One sec. One sec."

Her face was pressed against the plexiglass table cover, and her arms were tight around the base.

"Darlin', I know this was rough, but—"

"Got it!" She pulled her hand from behind the table, a big ziploc of cash dangling from her fingers.

"Jesus H, Jen! In an hour this place is gonna be crawling with security and any quiet cop that happens to be hanging around. Now you wanna pinch from the dead?"

"So, this place is gonna be crawling with assholes in an hour, right? You think them finding something like this is going to make it any less suspicious?" I didn't have an answer to that, and she knew it, so she went on. "Anyone who knows about this isn't on the up and up, so they're not telling anyone, and it not being here just makes him more of a sad tourist."

"But—"

"But nothing. I don't do this shit for the love of it... or the god damned art, like some lying rich girl on a rebellious streak. It's all about money, Phil. I saw that stack back there from the first step into the room, and it's not sticking around there waiting for housekeeping to scoop it away. You be as much of an angel as you want. I don't eat trau-

ma for free."

I couldn't begrudge her that. She walked all business to the door and I gave one more look around. Nothing seemed amiss, short of the corpse I guess, but I couldn't clean that with a bit of toilet paper. I gave Jen a reassuring smile, opened the door, and out we went.

As I shut the door, I nearly told Jen to put on the typical, disappointed, crying wife, but when I looked over she was already on it. The consummate pro. I went for tipsy husband, so I took on a wobble that wasn't bad enough to cry for assistance but had just enough to stop people from wanting to get involved.

We took the elevator down, Jen whispering nothing into my ear and moving her arm as though she was thoroughly sick of it, like most significant others dealing with a gambler, shocked but not hysterical, and I just swayed lightly. If you want to be invisible to the casino, that's the way to go. The whole time I was counting off the pros and cons of going to Giordano about it as soon as we hit the boards. As the doors opened, I threw

my arm over her shoulder, the bad tailor cut of the shoulder on my shirt bunching up to block her face just enough from the passerby.

The problem was, if I went to Giordano, I would probably have to talk to Pauly first. Pauly was a fat fuck, but he was just dumb enough to be dangerous. People like that couldn't be trusted to follow orders like clockwork, they got erratic or they got sloppy. I mean, just last time I saw him he was just lounging around like a lump of shit, playing with that little metal tube. The metal tube that definitely could have been an inhaler tube, come to think of it. Fuck.

As we made it through the gambling floor, I made sure to tell Jen how well she was doing. Couldn't have her cracking up now. All the while, I was keeping my eyes out. Two pieces of security were in my field of view but one was helping an old man with his scooter and the other was hitting on a cocktail waitress. At the exit, I took another look down the bank of slots and saw two Italians right out of a seventies fashion magazine walking toward the elevators. Could be nothing, but anything that it might be wasn't good.

BETTER LIVING
THROUGH BLOODSHED

I pushed open the door to the boardwalk, my heart hitting ribs hard enough to bruise, and the humid, thick air pressed me back, trying to trap me in this tomb of extravagance.

We cut upbeach toward the dark, and quiet, and freedom. Across from a five-for-twenty-bucks t-shirt shop, a pier, long forgotten in the midst of construction, sat in darkness. It had been at least five years since a hammer had been swung on the structure, and all of the 'coming soon' signs were tattered and bleached from the salt and sun.

I pressed myself through a gap between the warning fence and boardwalk rail to check that there was enough distance and helped Jen in behind me. All around us, a rotting playground sat. The carousel rested, with horses on buckling rails; the free-throw game waited with its net rotted away and rim sagging; the particle-board of the shooting gallery had bloated and warped everything into the point of a drowned body.

Past the games and 'employees only' sign, we hit the end of the pier, littered with chunks of pylon, steel, and scrap wood. I grabbed a chunk of rebar and hooked the ball-gag and cuffs to it

(that's the nice thing about bondage gear, it has its own attachment points) and tossed it off of the end of the pier. As it sank into the churning sea, Jen broke, grabbing me tight and sobbing into my shoulder. I held her there, the dark sea crashing against the rotting pier, and let her make her peace.

The walk home to Jen's was quiet in a way that only prolonged time with a corpse will do, and I couldn't figure out anything to say as she opened the door.

"Look, Jen," I started anyway.

"I'm fine."

"Seriously, tonight was—"

"I know." She stepped out into the light and her eyes weren't all glossy-wet, but business through and through. "You're always pulling this hard guy stuff, being cold and distant, like some fucking statue, but do you know what happens when you hang out next to a statue for too long? You start to become one yourself. I wasn't freaking out because of the body, I was freaking out because I wasn't, because I had turned so much into you. That's not something I want to be."

I stood there with fuck all to say to that, just

wavering shocked inside like a rot-gut drunk, as the door shut in front of me without so much as a goodnight.

I staggered into George's with eyes that were screaming for a bed and a back that felt like it was made of rusty sewing needles. Susie had headphones like a halved bowling ball over her ears and eyes locked on something under the counter. I poured some hot water over my tea, with a hand shaking so little specks of water hit my skin; the tingle burn doing nothing but waking flesh that felt like an old tire covering me.

I don't think Susie looked up as she slapped down some change, I was too busy eyeing the plate window without a real reason why, but also too many reasons why. My guts felt like they had washing machine parts mixed in and my head felt all dried bones in the desert. At the door was another loony note at a time when I couldn't handle another loony note, but I still bothered to throw it into my pocket as I opened the shop for another day.

It was cave quiet as I tried the neon and noth-

ing happened, not a peep of awful club mixes, but just as I was sure that Angelo had headed back to Philly, there was a low grind of wood on wood from above me. I made my way past the stations, picking up the little mini-bat from the counter as I got to the back door. The quiet of a shop, like a forgotten house, smothered me as I reached for the handle and found it open. I kept to the edge of the stairs to keep the creak away, and worked up the darkness, at the head of the stairs a sickly light more repulsive than the dark.

At the apartment entrance, bat cocked for a quick shot to the face, I found Angelo, head bowed, shirtless with humped shoulders, at the little circular table of the kitchen. If it wasn't for the steady lift of his back, I would've thought him dead. I dropped the bat down and made a slow walk to the table, making sure that my footsteps were heard.

"Hey, Ang," I said. "What's going on?"

All of the curtains were drawn, with just a little slice of life shining through a gap at Angelo's back. A little pile of white sat at his side, with a fallen glass leaking beer into the pile. In the sink,

a pile of Chinese takeaway boxes sat with roach babies scurrying about.

"Jimmy's gone," he said, with a catch in his throat.

"Who?" I felt like an asshole asking, but that's about all that you can ask in that situation.

"Jesus Christ, Phil Boy." He started to rise from his seat, arm reaching for the bottle on the counter, and tumbled onto the tabletop.

"I got it, I got it."

I grabbed the bottle and searched the cupboards for a pair of glasses, settling for a speckled jam jar and a coffee mug that a roach ran out of. Angelo rose when I smacked the bottle down and grabbed the coffee cup, leaving me glad I didn't have to choose. I poured two fingers of knock-off Frangelico into each and stood across the table from him.

"My cousin," he said, pouring the sugar-rot into his mouth. "They found him dead in a room last night."

My spine tried to go all jello at that, but you never can let your nerves get the better of you, even if you are a sleepless hour away from a coma, peo-

ple die every hour in this city. "What happened?"

He lifted the glass again, his pale tongue working around the inside of it for any last drop. "Don't you worry, Phil Boy. I'll find 'em."

"So," I lit a cigarette to clear my throat, "you lost me there, Ang." Even though I was getting surer every second that I couldn't lose him if I was blind and deaf.

"Jesus." He splashed some of a big pour into his glass. "What I'd give for a paisan from the city."

"Is there anything I can do?"

The liquor ran in tan rivers between the folds of his cheeks. "No, Phil Boy, no." He chuckled a chuckle full of graveyard dirt. "That frocio is walking on borr'd time." His head started to nod against his pillow-plump palm.

My guts sank so low, I thought they would squish when I took a step.

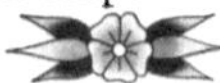

There was more of a chance that I'd get a lap dance from the pope than Angelo would be up to check on the shop that day, so it was like falling into a cloud as I landed on my couch. I pulled the smokes out of my pocket, and the little note land-

ed on my stomach; after lighting up and taking a big drag, I picked it up, ready to crumple, when a single word peeked out from within the folded paper. 'BODY' was scrawled in the same rambling lettering of the last few days. Am I impulsive? Sure. Am I rash? On occasion. Spiteful? My cup runneth over. But none of those so much as to let my fist close on that sheet of secrets.

'QUESTIONS GOING ROUND ABOUT THE BODY. MEET ME AT TONY'S. NOON. BE THERE. HA'

Wasn't this a turn like a corkscrew up the ass. Maybe the loony wasn't as loony as I thought. That, or I was crazy as a shit-house fly now, so it was all checking out. Either way didn't bode well. Noon, huh? I looked up at the old clock, half its frame lost to time, on the wall. Ten-thirty. Well, fuck me.

After beating the wrinkles from a half-decent shirt, I donned the full half-decent attire and laced up a recently-shined pair of boots. If you're gonna walk into an unknown situation, you might as well do it looking good. I didn't have time to send out laundry, so I'd have to hope for a dim cor-

ner of Tony's. I tucked the clip of my knife into a belt loop at my back since, even if he did know something, crazies know things sometimes. At the mirror, I checked my collar to be even, checked my eyebrows to be doing the same.

It was eleven-fifteen by the time I left the house; I said I dressed well, not fast. It was that cool humid out that puts the old fucks into a hospital. A light mist kicked up on the ocean winds that would have made an umbrella impossible either way. The Puerto Rican fellas were nowhere to be found, but their cars still looked like they'd come out of a time capsule from the eighties.

I cut across the parking lot where Tim's horrid visage has swayed me onto this path, and down the alley that had set the hook. All of these places were no different than they had been last month, or a year before, or ten, but they were different for me in perpetuity, just as countless places had been for countless others. Shit, probably these very places had become forever-changed for innumerable others.

At the outer doors, I checked that my blade was in place. At the inner doors, I closed my eyes

200

for a couple of beats to get them ready. It was go-time, baby.

The comfort-dark that you look for in a place like Tony's met me and, while I would usually love the acclimation to dismal, I was glad that I had let my eyes adjust in advance. I scanned the hobbled heads of old timers down the bar, at the booth closest to me the shoulder of a slumberer could be seen next to a pizza going cold. I was midway through the argument as to whether I should leave or sit down for a beer when a beckoning hand guided me over to the farthest booth.

A smarter man, more concerned with his self-image, would say that within an instant the notes all made sense, but they didn't. I plopped myself down and still had no idea who the fuck had been orchestrating these cryptic lines. The knife dug into my back, so there was small comfort.

He was somewhere near my age, well-dressed and well-shaved. I could still smell that chemical-cologne blend of the salon coming off of his hair. I guess the ignorance radiated from me because, before I could master a word from my fiberglass

mind, he said, "Don't remember me, do you?"

I was left thunderstruck, because I'm pretty sure that at that point thunder could have literally struck, however it is that sound can strike, and I wouldn't have noticed. "Sorry, it's been a long..."

"Hector Arroyo," he said, reaching out a hand with a bejeweled frog on a tan finger. The name was sparking something down toward the base of my skull, but nothing bubbled up. "Sophomore English—" It clicked. "And every year in some class or another before that."

Hector Arroyo, HA. Alright, that cut back a bit of loony.

"Shit, Hector, you were..."

"Weiner Loving Beaner. Yeah, I'm not even Mexican, so the nickname doesn't even make sense."

"I was gonna say a nice kid."

"I hoped you were. Never know back home, though."

The waitress pulled herself up, with that strange energy that a Tony's waitress always seems to muster, and asked, "What'll ya have dears?"

Hector started that hand wave that always

means nothing but hate from the servers when I ordered a couple of lagers and shots for us.

"I don't drink shots," Hector said.

"Today you do," I said. "If you plan on walking out with all of your tendons." I was tired of games, tired of mincing about, tired of this whole fucking circle. I placed my blade calmly on the table, running my finger over the surface.

"Drinks, fellas," the waitress said, without looking anywhere that she didn't have to, and slid the glasses in front of us.

"So what the fuck is going on?" I asked.

"You weren't so short with people back then."

"Well, I didn't have to get to a bar by noon back then," I said with a grin.

"You're not as cute as you think." He took his shot and smacked down the glass. "Lucky for you, Giordano is a lot less cute."

And, like it or not, there was the hook.

I took my shot, which burned like Vesuvius' asshole, and looked him straight in the eye. "How do you know Giordano?"

"In my line of work, I know a lot of people in a lot of places," he said, tapping the edge of his ring

on the empty glass. "More importantly, I know a lot of things about a lot of people that they would prefer no one knowing."

"And why should I trust that any of these things you know aren't just a bunch of bullshit?"

"Like I just said, I know a lot of things. One of those being the barrel Giordano has you over and, more importantly, the fact that he made sure you don't have a damned soul to go to to help you off of it."

He knew about the body, he knew about my being persona non grata on the streets, so I didn't have many reasons not to believe him. I also didn't have many reasons to trust him.

"So, if you're so close with Giordano, why should I believe you'd want to turn on him."

He eyed me for a long second, gears turning quick behind the eyes.

"The beaner part might have been wrong as wrong could be, but the other half of the nick-name wasn't. I let that slip once, and Giordano hasn't let me forget it since. You've met him and his, I'm sure you can understand how the jokes go."

BETTER LIVING
THROUGH BLOODSHED

"Alright, so you're queer. Why don't you just tell him to fuck off with the jokes if it bothers you so bad?"

"That's how you get this." He brought his other hand up over the edge of the table. The splint was dinged and scratched, the padding stained where it pressed against the purple and green skin of his pinky. It looked like there was an attempt to set the break, but the finger was still twisted at an unnatural angle.

"Jesus H, that's—"

"That's nine days tied to the radiator after Pauly had his fun with me. Just enough time for the nerves to die and the bone to start setting."

"Christ," I said, "imagine if you told him you weren't white."

That got a bit of a laugh out of him. Shit was getting a bit heavy and I was already carrying enough. I lifted my beer, gave him a cheers and took down half. It was a bit early, but in for a penny.

"So, what's the plan?" I asked and waved over the waitress for another round.

"The stereotype he is, Giordano loves a card

game," he said.

He went over the plan, and it seemed simple enough. Simple is good, anything that veers from simple is another way that the plan can get fucked. Giordano hit the high roller poker tables once a month, that once this month coincidentally being that night, and usually stayed until at least one in the morning. So, while he was trying to swing his out-of-town dick at other out-of-towners, we'd work a two-pronged attack. I'd get one of my girls to sidle up to Giordano when he was at the little bar outside the gaming floor, as he was apparently wont to do. At the same time, Hector would, after the pat down that even he received, head up to Giordano's office with a well-prepared suit coat. My girl would cozy up with Giordano at the table, while a plant would play hard then fold, making her the good luck charm. Hector would slice the lining of his coat and pull out some bags of dope, paper-thin compressed, and little baggies, and get to work. With a big smooch, my girl would slip a couple of dope baggies into Giordano's suit pocket. Hector would leave a memento of a past job of Giordano's, namely a severed finger, in the draw-

er on top of the baggies. After the game, my girl would head into the pisser, call a certain member of Atlantic City law enforcement, who had a tendency to always want his dick to get wet during a lap dance and a real drive to move up in the department, about Giordano trying to sell her dope (no name for him, just a detailed description) and word that he'd been bragging about all of the dope in his office. Hector, on his way out of the office, would call a couple of reporter friends about the tip, and they'd be waiting outside of the casino and the office. Bing, bang, boom, Giordano's radioactive.

"And what am I doing during all of this?" I asked.

Hector slid a set of car keys across the table. "On game nights, he always keeps fifty grand in the trunk, just in case he runs low. Level 4-C, black Mercedes. Wait for your girl to make contact in the phone booth by the boardwalk ramp. Once she does, you call me, and we both move."

I liked it. It was a little busy, but jobs are always at least a little busy, it just depends on how many gears you had to work around. You can't expect

point A to B when you're working outside of the realms of legal. Probably not even inside of them. There was a little nagging question, though.

"What's the cut on the cash?"

The corners of his mouth turned down, his eyebrow rose. "It's all yours. I get payed plenty."

"Then, where's the meet?"

"The Ocean View at nine tonight. I'm guessing your girl is one of the dancers?"

"How'd you guess?"

"I know things about people."

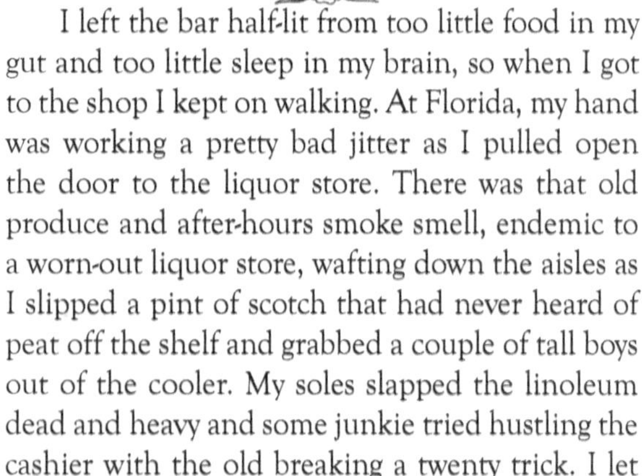

I left the bar half-lit from too little food in my gut and too little sleep in my brain, so when I got to the shop I kept on walking. At Florida, my hand was working a pretty bad jitter as I pulled open the door to the liquor store. There was that old produce and after-hours smoke smell, endemic to a worn-out liquor store, wafting down the aisles as I slipped a pint of scotch that had never heard of peat off the shelf and grabbed a couple of tall boys out of the cooler. My soles slapped the linoleum dead and heavy and some junkie tried hustling the cashier with the old breaking a twenty trick. I let

him try to work his slimy brain for a minute or two in rocking jerks and stutters, before I took two fingers from the hand holding the scotch and jerked his collar damned near to the floor. It's a cold world kid, and nothing gives a chill like a tired brain with a taste for the sauce.

Old crater-arms was yammering some whining attempts at a threat as I carefully counted out my cash and handed it over to the Filipino child behind the bullet-proof glass, and headed out the door. The sounds of the slamming door and a waft of rot followed me out and I turned on my heels. Junkie Joe nearly landed on his ass, but rose with that opiate-Nosferatu that a spike in the arm tends to grant. His tooth-occasioned mouth started to move, but I cut him short.

"I know I fucked up your game, kid, but today isn't your day. Move along and try another joint."

"Man, I just need some change. How 'bout you help me out, man. See, I just need change for this twenty, see? So, why don't you break it for me?"

"I'm not in the market for fake twenties, or giving thirty in change. Kick rocks and try some tourist."

He tried getting hard at that point, as every junkie in the history of the world has falsely thought themselves capable of. He pressed his chicken-bone chest against mine and cocked his head all movie-scary. "How 'bout you just give me what's in your wallet then, man?"

I lifted the bottle of scotch to just under his chin and didn't bother trying for a look. "Alright, kid. I know you're looking for a fix," I said casually, tapping his chin with the cap of the bottle. "But, I'm a man with places to be. So, if I have to put these bottles down, the only fix you'll get is from an IV for the next two months."

He stared long, trying to get a read, unable to comprehend that I was trying to tell him on the level. I saw some poor decision working through his Swiss cheese brain, and gave his remaining teeth a crack with the edge of the bottle. As he gave a grab for those sad pieces of enamel, I asked him, "Are we done here?"

He nodded and I turned away before I was too tempted to give him a kick that would show him what a real hard man was like.

I unlocked the shop, popped on the lights

BETTER LIVING
THROUGH BLOODSHED

that still decided to work, and went to the back of the shop, where the dirty room was located. I poured myself half a pint of beer and another half of scotch into the glass, and flopped down into the station. These were the Wild West days, and I was happily every villain from every spaghetti western. No one checked your alcohol level, these were the times for those rough enough to live them. I took a sip of that bemoaned concoction and felt the vice ease up on my brain. A tramp stamp came in and I mindlessly did it, then a pair of feathers on wrists that tried some argument that I barely heard but talked them out of.

While I was finishing up, some lump of muscle with a crew cut and a cheap suit took a slow stroll past the shop window, eyeballing everything inside, with a particular affinity for me. He was in too good shape to be local law, maybe out-of-city off-duty down for the day, but he definitely had that cop feel to him. Running through the after-care spiel, he made another pass, and I was just tipsy enough to make eye contact clearly enough to be noticed at a hundred yards. He didn't turn his head or hurry off to another dirty window, but

cracked a smile made of arsenic and casually pointed a roll-of-quarters-finger at me before tapping his watch.

The day died off after that, and I was left to my thoughts as the minutes ticked. I called Jen on the shop phone and told her the gist and, with a bit of trepidation, she agreed. As far as upstairs went, I didn't hear a creak or groan or explore for myself. The mystery man never made another appearance, but the message had been received.

At the end of the night, I felt a bit more comfortable with the plan, no matter who Giordano sent down to hurry me along, it wouldn't change anything. If anything, it might help. Let him think I was shaking scared on the ropes and hustling hard with every fiber of my being. You don't expect an offensive from someone that doesn't have a second to piss, let alone plan, so I locked up and headed down Pacific with my head dropped down from any prying eyes.

I headed through the main doors of The Ocean View, ignoring the remonstrations of the bouncers as I dodged the cover, and flopped myself down on a booth.

BETTER LIVING
THROUGH BLOODSHED

Jen hit the seat with a heave that rocked the booth and handed me a drink. "You alright?" I asked.

"I'm never alright around you, and I'm starting to realize that's probably a good thing to understand," she said.

"We can talk about all of that when this is done, darlin'."

I took note of the fact that Hector was still nowhere to be found. The dancers made their rounds and writhed on the pole, the rubes threw their money. I sipped at the drink, trying to keep my cool, as two fellas made their way in and sat at the bar, where no regulars sat. Looking like they just raided the wardrobe from the Blues Brothers, they weren't exactly inconspicuous.

Jenny kept talking and I managed to take in a few words as I glanced around the club. The two fellas at the bar eyeballed me in a way that made my ass pucker. Something was off. Most of the dancers kept a far radius.

Some North-Jersey-club-hit slid its way onto the crackling speakers as Desiré, one of the servers

working her way up to the fabled pole, came over to our booth. "Someone called for you," she said. It didn't take more than a beat of the lazy bass drum for me to realize the rest of the information wouldn't be forthcoming without the aid of my wallet. Oh, how quickly things were changing. I pulled out a ten and sat it on her little tray. "Someone called and said, um, you forgot something at lunch, or, wait... yeah, 'You left what you need at lunch'. I don't know how you could leave something at lunch, besides your lunch." Good thing she's cute.

I brought my mouth in close to Jen's ear, since every damned wall in the city seemed to have ears, and told her to giggle before I went on to tell her where I was heading, and that she should hop on a jitney in an hour to meet me at the casino. James and Jerry Bond over at the bar were doing their best to look casual, but I caught the occasional glance from the slightly dumber looking of the two. I told Jen I was going to hit the head, and asked her to get us two black and tans.

I waited at the entrance of the hall to the bathroom and, once Jen got a read on who I was

talking about and corralled them at the bar and started throwing on the charm, I made a quick walk to the door. Outside wasn't exactly Times Square, so I couldn't drag my feet about it. At the end of the building, I found a hole in the chain link and slid through with only a dozen or so little tears to my jacket.

The pair of bums were still over by the same burning trashcan, as though I'd just entered some timeless trap. I guess I must have come up on them in a bit too much of a hurry, because the one picked up an old piece of wood at my approach, but the Danny one seemed to have a bit better memory and calmed his pal down. Still, they were both a bit suspicious when I got up to them.

"Hey pal, I don't got that twenty you gave me. I spent it on food. I swear," Danny said.

"I don't give a shit if you spent it on a neutron bomb. There's another ten in it for ya if you haven't seen me. Ya dig?"

He looked over at the other fella for decision-making, and I guess they must have been hard up, because with a shrug he said, "Sure."

It wasn't a second too soon, because as soon

as I pressed into a shadowy corner of the lot, the Bond Twins came over to the fence and called Danny over. I couldn't hear a word, but they asked him something, Danny gestured around all crazy-like for an eternity, and eventually they got frustrated enough to storm off. Shit's weird when you can rely on a couple of guys like this more than people you've known for years.

I palmed off a twenty to him for a job well done, found another gap in the fence away from Pacific, and made my way on the long way west. The city could get pretty cold when you're dodging eyes, and I was damned near freezing. The wind whipped the shredded tatters of an old freebie paper around my ankles, a siren echoed off the rotting cement spine of the casinos, and I pulled one of the last smokes from my crumpled pack.

Short of a few places that were good enough to still drag along, Arctic was the little street that never was. Lights died early in the windows of the houses pressed tight together, traffic never was what it was through the rest of the city, and a thousand dirty hands did a thousand dirty deals in every nook along the asphalt. Eyes peeped out from

BETTER LIVING
THROUGH BLOODSHED

between blinds, and the president himself could scream himself hoarse for help without a door cracking open, like some long-isolated civilization. Every other property was a garage with its dingy parking lot, and its gaping doors with a little dim light hidden somewhere deep inside; the perfect kind of place to get disappeared into.

Still, just as it had with everyone else in the city, I hoped that the street had been wiped from the thoughts of the prying eyes that I was itching to avoid. At the corner of Stenton, one of those little streets that try with every bloodthirsty gasp to hold onto 'old Atlantic City', I was close enough to feel some sense of security, but smart enough to know better. Deep alleys that had long since become homes for old, dead cars, piles of broken furniture, weeds grown to trees, or illegal doorways into illegal basement apartments, were shadowy gouges between every other house. At the risk of being more noticeable, I figured heading down the center of the damned street was the safe option. Anyway, traffic would be shooting from in front of me instead of behind. I guess Stenton had one thing going for it.

Zachary Von Houser

I roosted up under the overhang of some half-rate barber shop across from Tony's, lit another smoke, and put my patience to work. The usual cast of nondescript cars rolled by, old timers teetered in sober and teetered out a little less sober, a broken down wino snored on a bench out front and just kept on snoring. If the Bond twins had known where I was going and headed right over, they would already be inside, if not, then there was no way to know if they'd ever get here. Things had gotten a bit too fucked to be anything but as safe as safe was possible, but there was only so long I could wait if the job had any hopes of working through that night. I crushed my smoke under my shoe, took a damned big, closed-eyed breath, and crossed the street.

The balding heads at the bar had replaced other balding heads, different asses warmed the worn vinyl of the booths, I couldn't tell if it was the same sleepy-head napping at the booth closest to the door but the pizza had long since gone. The Bond boys weren't anywhere to be found, but neither was Hector, and my hand went to check the tuck of my knife. Sinatra was belting out some bebop shit about a long-gone dame and I must have been looking like a lost puppy because the bartender was eyeballing me from along the bar. I'd just ordered a drink to take the attention off me, and was thinking over making a break, when the bathroom door let out a little shriek and Hector came out drying his hands on the sides of his pants.

"You had me a bit worried there, kid," I said as I slid into the booth.

"You weren't exactly keeping a low profile today. So, it seemed best to err on the side of caution."

I was about to ask him just what the shit he was getting at when he went on. "Nearly bludgeoning an addict on Pacific Avenue is far from 'low profile'."

"Yeah, you've got me there," I said, fighting back the urge to bitch about pressure and such. Life is nothing but pressure and such, so you'd better adapt or fall under the force of it all. "He was fucking asking for it, though." I wasn't going to ask him how he knew. 'I know a lot of things'.

"They usually are, but this is hardly the time

to indulge ourselves."

"Point taken." I took a sip of my drink and eyed the dining room.

"Matty and Dean haven't been in." Hector eyed my drink with no small amount of contempt. "Unless, that is, you're looking for a dinner to go with that drink."

"It'll take more than this to get me going," I said and took another drink, more out of spite than being parched. "Does any of this change the plan?"

"Not unless you can think of a reason."

"Not a one. If you're done with the sass, grab my phone while you're up there."

"Pauly took it?"

"At least I'm not the first idiot."

I called Jen at the club and told her we were still on.

I can't think of a longer wait than on that cold night by the boards. The fresh pack of smokes I'd grabbed on the way dwindled under my feet until I wondered if it'd burn through my sole, and every joint in my body yearned for something warm to drink. Ocean-heavy clouds rolled in and on toward the mainland, shoobies passed into the casino in ones and twos and gaggles, and somewhere in the dark a ship's horn sounded.

The dead-eyed look that Jen had given me—like she'd never seen a countenance such as mine—when we met on the boards had bled out more than a little of my heart, but she had had the kindness to dress the part and looked ready for business, so there really wasn't shit that I could say. I gave her a quick brief of how Giordano would probably be looking, which was met with a look like I was teaching a college kid their ABCs, and was about to offer her my blade when she held up her little purse like a palm reader. My mind was scrambling for something new to say, which was a previously unknown feeling around her, when she said, "Alright then," and turned on her heel for the casino entrance.

After an eternity of wait, the suddenness of the ringer shook something deep in my chest, and the smoke fell from between my fingers. "Hey," I said.

"It's no good," Jen said, all tinny through the

cacophony of the casino.

"What's not? He didn't go for you?"

"I wouldn't know. He's not here."

A lead flail wedged itself into the base of my gut without the intention of moving.

"He's not at the tables anywhere?"

"I pick out men for a living, Phil. If he was here I would have seen him."

It was past the point of things going south, and damned near to the border.

"So, what do you want me to do?" Jen asked.

"Head home, I'll meet up with you tomorrow. Stay safe."

As soon as the line went dead, I dialed the number Hector had given me. It rang a few times, and a strange garbled noise came through. Thinking there must be something wrong with the connection, I hung up and tried again.

"Please leave a message for—" I gave it another go. "Please leave—" I gave it another ten minutes of chain-smoking before I tried again for a ring that wouldn't come.

It was time to put emergency orders into action. Not a soul could be seen on the boardwalk,

as though everyone on the island had gotten the memo that everything had gone tits up. Everyone besides me.

I dropped onto my ass and under the rail, being half a block from the closest ramp, and onto the sand. The wind was howling across the moon-grey sand, and the surf was battering the world into oblivion. I stopped under the boards and made a hunched walk downbeach. Who knows who was in Giordano's pocket, at this point it could be anyone, and the last thing I wanted at that moment was to be spotted on one of the casino's, or John Law's, boardwalk cameras.

At a few spots, the sand had built up under the boardwalk to the point that I had to crawl on hands and knees, my back brushing the tar-caked bottoms of the boards; at other times it had eroded away to the point that I was splashing through sopping sand an inch beneath the sea. Try as I might, from this weird perspective, I couldn't keep track of just where I was until I heard a familiar chunk of one of the looping ads that blared from the casinos.

When a rant about the best steaks in town

slithered down to me through the cracks in the boards, I slid down a buildup of sand that had me army crawling with barely enough room to breathe and caught my breath for a second before brushing away the sand. I straightened out my clothes, lit a smoke, and headed up and across the boards. My guess was off, and I was a block short of where I wanted to hit Pacific, which would have been on the far side of the shop. I could probably make it work, though, with a little luck. Something that I was running low on.

The alley was dark and littered with ankle-breaking halves of old chairs, long-dried five-gallon paint buckets, and broken mops. I kept my hand cupped around the cherry of my smoke and away from any waiting eyes, with one slow step at a time. On some of his lazier nights, Angelo kept a key in the drainpipe for the call girls, and I just hoped that he'd been preemptive after the last time. I dug my fingers into the rusty, wet recess, and let out a heavy sigh.

I opened the door as quiet as a cheap door on a crooked building could open, and locked it behind me, dropping the key into my pocket.

BETTER LIVING
THROUGH BLOODSHED

The shop was dark, and that's how it stayed, as I crouched low and made my way toward my station. At the half-wall between my station and the waiting room, I reached under my sink and grabbed the cheap bag that someone had left there months before. My machines and power supply were hastily tossed into the bag, along with my sketchbook and pens, and a plastic bag of mixed tubes and needles that had been collecting here and there for the last month or two. If I was going to hole up somewhere, it was better to do it with a means of income, even if I was making my scratch in someone's kitchen. Either way, I wasn't leaving my machines to rust or get pinched by some seasonal prick during the summer. They were my babies after all.

I braved a quick glance over the counter and the silhouettes of a couple of guys were planted, leaning against the front window. At the far edge, the big taillights of a big car idling at the curb. I placed the keys on my station, reached back to the empty place at the back of my belt where the knife had been, and swallowed hard, its razor-sharp reassurance lost forever somewhere under the boards.

Zachary Von Houser

I thought over the Kley for a minute, but I had no idea where I would be roosting up, so for the time being it would have to fend for itself.

Back out the door and down the alley, I went back to the boardwalk and hurried a few blocks farther downbeach before I cut off again. I just needed to hole up somewhere for a bit, just a few weeks or a month, until I could get things back into order, get a line of defense together. But there was something I needed to do first.

My defenses fought to keep sharp against the cloying familiarity as I made my way down the block and up those dogleg brick stairs. I pulled out my sketchbook, wrote quickly, tore the page in half, and folded piles of cash into each half. On the front of one improvized envelope, I wrote Mary, the other Jen, and slid them both through Mary's mail slot. My every instinct, every synapse screaming for comfort and regularity tempted my knuckles to the door, but that would have to wait. They already knew where Mary lived, it wouldn't go well if they found me there. When she read the note, she'd know to go over to Jen's. She could hunker down there for a bit until things blew over.

BETTER LIVING
THROUGH BLOODSHED

I knew I was fooling myself to think that she would do that, would leave the only home she'd ever had, but thinking on the fly is never foolproof. I'd give her a ring when I found whatever rabbit warren I was going to hide away in. Hopefully, I'd be able to convince her then.

Until that point, the street was calling.

So, here I was slinking out of town in the middle of the night, with fuck all besides the clothes on my back, some machines and supplies in my bag, and a few bucks in my pocket. The street was still jam-packed with the late-night going-to's and leaving-from's cars in long lines of lights shining into my eyes. A group of kids were hassling some passerby next to the old convention center in a way that had me getting nostalgic. Age, exhaustion, or the looming loss of home and everything I'd ever known, I'm not sure what had me feeling for the little dickheads, but whatever it was had me thinking instead of paying attention, which is what I should have been doing.

I didn't even notice the car pulling up until it was creeping along my side at the same pace as me.

227

Zachary Von Houser

I slowed down, and on went the brakes, quickened my pace and they hummed right along with me. In a situation like that your balls pull in tight and your heart sinks low, like they're trying to meet somewhere in the middle of your guts. At Bellevue Ave I stopped dead and they hit the brakes. Three directions to bolt didn't give me an advantage, but I was slightly less fucked by the odds.

The rear window rolled down, and an eczema-freckled hand reached out and drummed on the door, and Angelo's face crept mournfully out of the gloom of the back seat. It wasn't the Italian mug that I really didn't want to see, but it still wasn't a pleasant surprise. His bag-ridden eyes were glassy from a cocktail or two, and the red spot on the front of his t-shirt told a tale of a recent pasta dish. The little gem on his pinky ring blinked in the streetlight as he continued his slow drumming.

"Ang..." I started as the passenger door opened and Pauly stepped out, the brief illumination showing Lucky Tom himself in the back seat. The fucking rat. "Angelo, I'm not sure what they told you—"

He put his palm toward me, like it was almost

too much effort to lift. "I've always been good to you, kid. I give you a job when no one else wants you. I make sure you're taken care of. I introduce you to people you never would have met in your sad little life on this shit island. And how do you repay me?" He shook his head in a way that I knew he'd practiced a million times since he first saw The Godfather. "What they did was business, all part of the game. I know it, everyone knows it. You didn't have to take the job, but you did, and what you did, kid, makes you responsible for Jimmy's death. And for you to take my cousin from me, after all I did for you? That's personal."

Pauly stepped toward me, a chrome pistol wedged tight between his gut and belt line, and gripped up the back of my arm.

"Don't worry, though," Angelo said with a slimy smirk spreading through his fatty folds. "I know you're not fully to blame. I'll be having a talk with that girly of yours. Maybe if she's real nice to me, I'll forget her part in all of this... for a little while."

Before I could take a step, the gun was in my ribs. I probably would have still gone for it, used

my last breath squeezing that fat neck shut, but I knew that I'd never make it to the car before a piece of lead ended up in my skull.

"Leave your bag," Pauly said. "This'll be quick."

The hot, bloated madness of blood jostled in the freeway veins of my hands, drumbeat rain stuttered across silty puddles, a dancing whistle bounced around the buildings, and the gotcha-smile of the city split my heart in two. Turns out, it sure is a clusterfuck of emotions that you get walking into a dark tomb alley with a piece of murderous metal digging into your muscles. There's that acid tingle in your nerves urging you to swing, those suicidal fucks; the dead weight in the base of your skull saying to just pack it in and get it done with where you are, like that's some great stand to take (you're still just a dead fuck at the end of the day, only a few feet to the left of where it was going down anyway); and the nagging impulse to try and reason, but murderers don't reason. A little down the alley, beneath a streetlight twitching out its last hours of work, something moved in an alcove of brick. Maybe salvation still existed, maybe provi-

dence was reaching a guiding hand down to me. I wouldn't need more than a second of distraction for Pauly and I'd be able to turn this all around. Maybe the taste of fate wasn't quite so bitter after all.

"Thank you, Pauly. Back to the car," Giordano said, stepping out into the light, and the taste of batteries slipped into my mouth.

"You got it, boss."

The pressure left my ribs, the wet slap of steps retreated back toward Pacific, and I was left with the rain, the night, and shit luck holding the handle for the trapdoor beneath my feet. Giordano circled around until I had my back a matchstick away from the wall, his cologne blocking the stink and rot and moldering of the alley

"I did what you said, so what's this all for?" I said, trying to straighten my spine into a steel rod.

"This?" He gestured around us. "Call it tying up loose ends, call it just for fun, call it this shit taste that uppity micks like you leave in my mouth." The little click of a blade slipping open came from his hand.

I gave a last, desperate glance down the alley

for any ray of hope, shit, I would even take a cop if any weren't crooked as hell, and saw Pauly's car pulling up; its long side blocking the entrance from one side to the other.

"I can see you trying to figure it out. How'd I know where you'd be," he said, but if this was gonna be my last few minutes, I wasn't going to help with his little fucking game.

Pauly got out of the car and leaned against the door, arm crossed across his fat gut. I couldn't make out his face from that distance, but I'm guessing there was a smug smile carved in that mashed potato face.

"Huh," he said. "Must not be it. How's about 'why isn't he at the Tidal Club'?" I must have flinched, I'm not sure because I didn't notice, but Giordano sure as fuck did. "Ah, there it is. Well, it's the same answer for both." He flicked his wrist, and a little splash came from the puddle at my feet.

I looked at Giordano first, as this rat-smile cut its way across his face, down the shoulders of his shark-skin suit, over the tie-pin with the little dago horn shining gold, the brown-leather shoes with the ugly European toe. I was stalling, because

232

nothing tossed toward me at that time in that place would be any good for me. A finger sat in the puddle, the skin where it had been attached to a hand puckered and constricting around the fleshy innards. Atop the silver band that hugged skin so tightly, spread a frog, the red and blue gems of its eyes sitting just below the surface of the water.

You need to keep an eye out for every bastard ever shat out into this world, but you especially have to watch out for a mean one trying to goad you on. So, it was with as much composure as I could collect that I said, "Where is he?"

"That's a tough one to answer, O'Niell. You see, I'm no expert on tidal currents, but from what I saw, the last of ten or so trash bags was falling over the rail of the bridge into this rat-fuck of a town." His thumb rubbed along the knurled handle of the blade. "Let's see if we can give you a little reunion." He took a step, a too-calm step, toward me when the stammering clink of glass on concrete came from just outside the reaches of the light.

"Ay yo," came a voice, something that I recognized from somewhere, but I was too focused on

the knife down at Giordano's thigh.

Giordano was looking cagey, obviously not accustomed to the unexpected, eyes darting, a thousand gears trying to fight a grain of sand out of their teeth. Stuck between a wall and a cold fuck with dead eyes and a blade is a pretty shitty place to be; stuck between a wall and a cagey fuck with unsure eyes and a blade is a fuck-ton worse. A new pair of Tim's splashed a puddle as they came into the light, the sharp snap of cigarettes being packed pulled Giordano's attention as well as mine, and a well-known face came into view.

"Beat it, mulignan," Giordano said.

"You got a light?" Q asked, pulling a cigarette into his mouth with his teeth.

"You hear me, darkie? Kick rocks."

"I'm just askin' for a light, old head."

"You're gonna be asking for an undertaker, you don't get the fuck out of here." Giordano turned toward him.

"Funny thing about shoobies, they come down here with this idea that they're the king, never seein' that there's already a mother fucker on the throne." He took a step closer and the blade

in Giordano's hand got twitchy. "It's all good, though. I'll get a light somewhere else." He let out a quick pair of high whistles, and everything moved fast.

At the end of the alley, windows on the second floor at either side slipped open. Pauly looked up, back and forth, like he was looking for rain. A pair of little flashes came at each dark window, choreography close. And two little meteorites came cascading down. One hit the roof of the car, with the smash of breaking glass, and flames ran across paint. The other shattered across the side of the car and, in an instant, Pauly was a dancing, screaming star. The car was blanketed in fire faster than I would have thought, the frame rocking on wheels as the occupants fought over whether to stay or go. It watched for a moment, trapped in the sublime, just like others standing beside me, but it's not too often that you're given a governor's reprieve. So, while the walls danced in the light of the flames, and the car turned into an oven, and Pauly's body popped and whistled with melting fat, I acted.

Giordano was on the ground before his head

could turn toward me, my shoulder catching just below his sternum as I brought us both down onto the asphalt. I was hoping to put the wind out of him, but an arm around my neck told me I'd missed the mark, a fist into my side confirmed it. I elbowed his hand away, and put two quick shots into his ribs, feeling that beautiful giving-way of bone breaking. The impact of the asphalt must have knocked me harder than I thought, because a warm slosh was splashing around in my head and my heart was hitting with heavy, slow thuds. He squeezed tight on my neck, bringing my face into his jacketed chest with more force than I would have expected, and the suffocation of damp silk against my mouth caught my chest. My finger snagged in the corner of his mouth and teeth came down onto my knuckle. Nothing but the pain-numb of adrenaline kept my finger locked into his mouth and, with that flap of wet flesh gripped tight in my fist, I brought his head up and crashed it back down into the pavement.

The arm around my neck was a limp noodle, metal tinkled at my side, and my vision swam as I pulled my head back and into cold air. Giorda-

no's eyes were squeezing open and shut and his mouth was moving like he was whispering some absolvement, my lungs were pulling deep and I felt like I was about to puke when I caught the glimmer from the corner of my eye. There wasn't some great, final statement from me to him, no heartfelt message, no shocking barb of wit, just a quick grab of the knife with my hand, a downward motion, and a twitching look of shock as the handle of the blade rose and fell from out of the center of his chest.

In hindsight, I could bullshit you and tell you that what happened next was cleaning up evidence, or being sure to leave no threat, but it was just for funsies. Just yanking the lever to the tension-floodgates of my mind. I pulled the blade from his chest, noticing the lack of expected spray, and drove it into each of his eyes a half-dozen times.

I stumbled to my feet, fighting back the bile coming up my throat and steadying the sea legs that seemed to have taken my balance. Q stood a few feet away, watching the flames ripple of the bare-metal car. I reached into my pocket and

pulled out the crumpled pack of broken cigarettes.

"I've got a light, you got a spare smoke?" I asked.

He tapped one out of the pack and handed it over as I passed him my lighter. While I lit mine, he let out a long plume of smoke, pointed at my shirt, and said, "he got you."

The first drag felt too good, so I closed my eyes for a second, keeping in the burn, before I looked down. The side of my shirt was pasted to my ribs red, and with each big breath, a new ring of shimmery wet was born from a little slit in the center. I tried to roll Giordano over, but I wasn't feeling particularly strong, and even from the right angle it's damned hard to wrangle the arms of a body out of sleeves. So, instead, I just took the blade, ran it quick around the shoulder of the jacket, and pulled the sleeve off of the arm, balled it up against my side, and buttoned my jacket to hold it in place.

I was staring out at the car again, the flames dying down, when a reminder crossed me. There was a second of hope, like for some reason my luck would have changed from a heap of shit, before

BETTER LIVING
THROUGH BLOODSHED

I saw the pile of charred plastic that was my bag, machines, and anything else that would help me start again.

"Ay, yo," Q said. "You best get goin' if you don't wanna wear some bracelets."

My head was nothing but fuzz from any number of things that had happened in the last few days, not to mention the dwindling blood trickling through me, so I didn't quite catch the point and instead stared at him with what I'm sure was the dumbest face a person could make.

"Them cameras over there," he said, pointing at the wall across Pacific and grabbing my upper arm, "can read the brand on the side of one of your smokes. They won't have no problem picking up your face talking to them dumb motherfuckers two minutes before they turned barbecue. Ya heard?"

It finally clicked, and I squeezed my eyes to force out the lingering fog on my senses. "What about your boys?" I pointed up at the dark vacancy of the windows.

"Them? Shit, they'll be bare rooms before the cops get here. Probably already are." He pulled out

another two smokes and lit them for us with my lighter. "Those young bucks been trained well."

I dug around in the pockets of my jacket and the tremor in my hands unnerved me. I'd have to check on this soon, but not before I got out of the jurisdiction. Eventually, I found what I was looking for, pulled out the little roll of cash that I had left, and tried pulling off some twenties.

"Nah, none of that shit," Q said. "Summer'll be here soon enough."

I gave him a quick fist bump and was about to go on my way, wherever that might be, when he cleared his throat. "I'll take that blade, though, if you're feeling generous."

I didn't even notice that I still had the blade open in my hand. "Shit, saves me a trip to the storm sewer." I slid the blade closed, felt the little click of the catch, and handed it over.

"I fuckin' love a trophy."

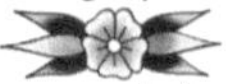

I made a circuit around the block and scrubbed my hands and wrists in the Caesars fountain until the water came away clean and chlorinated. Then it was a cut down Michigan, in the shadow of the

BETTER LIVING
THROUGH BLOODSHED

beckoning call of the hospital, which would mean a quick patch-up and quicker lockup, and a hasty right onto Atlantic with sanctuary in sight.

Johnny Law was waiting at the far doors, those pneumatic slips to six wheels of freedom, but he was one of those old fuckers just waiting out his months until retirement or a coffin. A few sad wretches sat or laid across the bent steel benches, none of them looking strong enough to stand, let alone kill for hire. Ticket machines lined the one wall, but I made for the windows, cashier's memories are give and take, but fingerprints on a screen aren't near as foggy.

A tagged and chipped print of the great state of New Jersey, with its multicolored lines winding routes through its expanse, showed how far you could go on a ticket; not where I wanted to go, but how far you could. I asked for a ticket to the northern-most point in an accent that wasn't Jersey, but wasn't quite anywhere else, just your usual America accent, the cashier seemingly amazed that anyone would have that much money left before they took a bus out of my soon-to-be-former town. Her calloused little stubs of fingers flipped through

pages of some yellowed binder, and a smoky voice grumbled in disgruntlese, before she came up with a number that probably had nothing to do with a pricing sheet. I pulled some bills from the center, where they were free of sticky red but did have some puddle sludge on the corner, and handed them over. Dull eyes shimmered the antithesis of bemusement, the damp bills went somewhere under the counter, and a little slip of paper and a nickel were slapped down in front of me.

"Thanks, sweetheart," I said, pocketed the slip, and headed for the far doors.

I'm not sure if the cool had kicked in that hard during the time I spent under those death-colored fluorescents, or if my adrenaline had finally shit the bed, but a chill crept stealthy into my marrow the moment that those second set of doors slid open before me. You had your usual groups of world-weary nomads lining up before each of those steel behemoths in varying states of decrepitude and exhaustion, and I posted up somewhere toward the center with a good view of the line of dead dark marquees, the doors to the terminal, and the far gate. Cologne, tobacco smoke, and

body odor wafted in the night air.

Down by the end, an engine rumbled into life, the marquee popped bright, and the crowd posted up snapped into attention. I ambled my way casual down to the end of the line and tried to keep as forgettable as possible. As I shifted slow-motion forward, as a crowd is wont to move, I checked my jacket and saw the little Rorschach bubbling up from my side, a drip hitting my shoe with a heavy thud. I pressed my hand in and played it cool up the steps. A cadaver back to life sat in the driver's seat and eyed me warily when I handed over the ticket.

"You sure you're on the right route, kid?" he asked.

"That's what she gave me," I managed to croak and, with a shrug from the driver, shuffled back to a seat near the back.

The doors hissed, there was a jolt as we reversed, and there I sat, shaking cold, leaving town like some rube, with a hole in my gut two inches wide.

Zachary Von Houser

www.ingramcontent.com/pod-product-compliance
Lightning Source LLC
Chambersburg PA
CBHW032248310726

48973CB00008B/2336